CW01426401

T.

David Brookes

The *RED BOAT*

SeaCrab Books

SeaCrab Books

This edition published

0830 hrs GMT on

17th September 2022

ISBN: 9798353288244

Dedicated

to my wonderful partner and friend

Susan,

*without whose kindness and support
this book would not have been possible*

Prologue

Five years ago, I was involved in several serious events due to bad choices. I began smuggling contraband cigarettes across the English Channel – which turned out to be hard drugs.

Two people I knew got their heads blown off with sawn-off shotguns – both weapons turned up with my fingerprints on them. I was framed. I was hunted by the police and by a group of ruthless killers. I narrowly escaped death several times and I was fortunate not to end up incarcerated in prison for the rest of my life.

My little boat – Beach Boy – was destroyed.
My sister and her 2 sons were kidnapped.
I received £50,000 from the media for my story.
I gave up smoking.
I sold up and moved to Norfolk.

Chapter 1

The toaster popped up. I nearly jumped out of my skin. I had been engrossed in reading an article in my daily newspaper about a man who had recently been arrested in St. Malo, France.

His name was Mark Hopkins. The toaster popped at the exact moment I read his name. A lot of time had passed since I had been involved in his murky, dangerous world and I had almost forgotten him.

The article described him as *'a drug smuggler and multiple murderer'* which was accurate. He had been a direct threat to my liberty and to my continued existence. He probably still was.

He had been arrested yesterday evening after a shoot-out with the French police, which resulted in the deaths of two cops and one of Mark Hopkins' associates – a man named Fred, to whom I had added the epithet 'Meathead' after having met him on several unpleasant occasions. I wouldn't be losing any sleep over his demise – I only regretted the fact that Mark was still alive.

Not just because I hated and feared the man but because once he was eventually dragged into court, I would be forced to give evidence against him in the witness box.

This in itself would give me great pleasure – the thought that I might finally see my nemesis brought to justice based on my own personal testimony. I would gain a sweet sense of justified revenge from this. No, the reason I felt a sense of dread creeping over me was that Mark Hopkins had the ability to wriggle out of very tight situations, usually by getting some other mug to take the fall on his behalf.

He was not a man who would allow people who were threats against him to rest securely in their beds. I feared he would be sending some unpleasant people to find me and eliminate me before any trial could get off the ground. He knew that my evidence was crucial to the prosecution's case regarding two murders he had committed in England, before he had dramatically escaped to France.

The fact that two French policemen had been shot while apprehending him, did not necessarily mean he had shot them. It was more likely that Meathead had decided to go out in a blaze of glory; he had an overdeveloped penchant for direct action.

He had also exhibited great loyalty to Mark Hopkins in the past – even before Mark had shown uncharacteristic compassion in return, by saving his life after Fred had been shot in a violent altercation amongst criminal colleagues during a frantic journey across the Channel to France, when they had managed to flee British justice.

I was hoping that Mark had shot at least one of the Gendarmes as it would mean the French police would have evidence against him for murder of a police officer.

This would lessen the importance of my evidence against him and might just make him reconsider the necessity of removing me as a witness – particularly as I had not actually seen him commit the killings – though he had admitted them to me and had been in possession of the murder weapons. I wouldn't be holding my breath. Mark enjoyed getting rid of people he didn't like and I was firmly in that category.

I took my toast from the machine and spread some butter and honey on it. The taste was bland. My tea tasted brown. I felt tired, though it was only 8am.

I slouched into the bathroom and half-heartedly brushed my teeth. I didn't like what I saw in the mirror. Beard getting trampy. More lines on face. Skin looking pale and yellowish. Eyes a bit starey.

"Fuck off you prick!" I barked to my reflection. He didn't answer, just looked angry and scared at the same time. I laughed. He laughed. The laughter was hollow.

Chapter 2

Bloxham St. Michael is a tiny hamlet, hidden away in a remote corner of Broadland, a non-metropolitan district situated in Norfolk with the lowest crime rate in the whole of the UK. It is also the most peaceful.

I moved here three years ago after selling my small 2 bed semi, in a faceless housing estate in Winchester, Hampshire.

I now lived in an even smaller, ramshackle cottage close to the River Bure. Apart from my dwelling, I owned a boat, a Land Rover, 5 shirts, 3 pairs of jeans and a couple of socks.

I spent a considerable amount of time lazing about on my untidy veranda which overlooked the river or pootling about on the Norfolk Broads in my boat, *Valerie II.*

I lived alone and intended to continue doing so. I sometimes grunted at my few neighbours but mainly I ignored them and they ignored me. It suited us that way.

There was a small boatyard nearby which was useful for mooring; when I needed work done on my boat; fresh supplies of grease; oil or general chandlery. The man who ran it was local born and bred and spoke with a cosy dialect which I had slowly become almost fluent in.

Norfolk people like to make pronunciation difficult for tourists. There are places like Costessey (Cossey), Wymondham (Windum) and Happisburgh (Hazeborough) throughout the county, named to separate locals from interlopers or Johnny-come-Latelies. The trick was to leave out the 2nd syllable - or most of it.

I loved it here: the self-contained personalities of the people; the primal nature of the landscapes; most of all the peace and quiet.

I particularly liked the fact that virtually no one knew where I was or who I had been. I was in hiding - on advice from Special Branch.

Following the attempts on my life; during my involvement with Mark Hopkins and his little tribe, I had given evidence which helped convict a man called Harries for murder; for the abduction of myself; for the kidnap of some of my family members: he had received a double life sentence.

I had not been the main prosecution witness in the case and the likelihood of any of his connections seeking me out for revenge was fairly low, according to the cops.

Hopkins was now in police custody in France - it would once again become important for him to eliminate me if he could. Special Branch had recommended that I 'move somewhere quiet and keep out of mischief'. I had taken their advice.

I had made quite a bit of money from media interviews and newspaper articles, which – along with the money I had obtained from the sale of my house in Winchester – had enabled me to buy my current little pied à terre as well as a very nice boat.

For the past two years, I had been preparing for the possibility that Mark Hopkins would appear back on my radar. Either Mark personally or some 'representative' operating on his behalf. My radar had now been alerted.

Not only was it Mark Hopkins I had to be wary of. There was a guy called Leo Thomas who was the uncle of Harries and more than likely a person high up in the drug smuggling business of which Mark Hopkins had been an integral part.

Thomas had once saved my life and rescued me from a watery grave after Hopkins' second attempt to kill me. His house had been searched for drugs, though none had been found. His nephew, Harries had been holding hostages in Thomas' house and had forced me at gun point to help him escape when the police raided the premises. Fortunately for Thomas, he was rich enough to employ a barrage of slick London lawyers and ended up with no charges being brought against him.

It was not likely that Thomas would attempt to have me assassinated as I couldn't give any useful evidence against him – quite the reverse – the fact that he had saved me from the water would help him rather than threaten him in any way. No, his reasons, if any, for taking care of me would be that if I gave evidence against Hopkins, then Hopkins was very likely to give evidence against Thomas in order to mitigate his sentence.

The police were pretty sure that Thomas would have a contract out on Hopkins to stop him talking, but after more than five years, they had been unable to get him – until the recent arrest of Mark Hopkins in France.

I sat in an old armchair on my veranda and watched some swans for a bit, before closing my eyes for a little nap I had planned. I was just nodding off when the phone rang, disturbing my serenity.

I made my way into the house and picked up the receiver.

"What?"

"Michael Garvie?"

"Who wants to know?"

"Jack Glaze". I was not happy to hear this and more than a little annoyed. I had expected this call to come at some point, now that Mark Hopkins had been arrested but a part of me had hoped that it would never happen.

"What kept you?"

"Sorry old chap" he couldn't hide a slight chuckle as he sensed my disappointment at his call. "I'm sure you're aware by now that the operation has started"

"I've seen the papers"

"That's good. I'm just giving you the official say so, old boy".

Ever since he had been moved from Special Branch to an offshoot of M.I.6 known as G10, Glaze had developed some very odd mannerisms, one of which was to call everybody 'Old Boy', 'Old Chap' or Old Bean'.

"That's very fucking nice of you, thanks for letting me know"

"You're very welcome, Michael. Are you clear about what you must do?"

"Of course"

"All your equipment and assets in place?"

"Yes"

"Right then Old Fella, let's get the party started"

"Up yours, Old Bastard". As I hung up, I could hear Glaze laughing. It must be nice to have something to laugh about.

I grabbed my keys and wallet, put on my green, army-style jacket, locked up my house, drove away from my cosy hideaway and entered a whole new world of pain.

Chapter 3

I left my Land Rover in an underground car park and ran up the stone steps which led to the main concourse of Norwich railway station. The place was quiet, the main London train having left just ten minutes before.

I walked to the office and bought a one-way ticket for Great Yarmouth. This was a local route and the two-carriage train was already waiting by the platform on the far left of the station.

I boarded the train and took a seat as far away from the other four passengers as possible – not for security reasons. For unsociable bastard reasons.

The journey took about an hour. I watched the wide, pastoral scenery, like something out of another age, pass me by as we moved slowly through Acle. There were windmills, cows, horses, streams, wide grasslands and the biggest horizons in the whole country on offer. My eyes enjoyed looking at it, though my mind didn't join in and my heart was too busy pounding to give a shit.

Things were about to get strange – and dangerous.

Since my initial involvement in the exciting world of smuggling, I had begun to experience a new dimension to my personality. It is often only when faced with genuine threats to your existence that certain primal parts of your psyche kick into life. Mine had kicked in strongly over the past few years.

I had also been forced to sign the Official Secrets' Act and received induction training from a shadowy military organisation which was part of G10 – itself a 'hidden' arm of M.I.6. It was all very cryptic and many of the procedures I had been taught to follow in 'special situations' still made little or no sense to me. Maybe this nonsensical nature was a method of confusing any enemy agents – it certainly confused me.

Why for example did I have to leave my vehicle in Norwich instead of driving the 19 miles to Yarmouth – which would have taken about 20 minutes? Instead, I waste over an hour getting a slow train – I also don't have access to a vehicle once I get there.

I had been approached a few weeks after my appearance in court. There was a plan being implemented, the aim of which was to gain knowledge of those mysterious people who were controlling the drug cartel from deep cover. The shadow people who gave orders and made payments to people like Mark Hopkins and (ex) Sergeant Liam Harries.

Harries himself had made some sort of deal – possibly gaining parole a bit sooner in the process. I had been told little about the content of any agreements but had been advised that information supplied by him to the secret service had enabled the current operation to move forward with considerably greater clarity and focus.

The key to the whole operation and the signal for me to 'Go Go Go' was the arrest of Mark Hopkins. My arrival in Great Yarmouth was the first step in a 'well organised and highly targeted undercover and military operation'. Or so I had been led to believe.

The train arrived early at Great Yarmouth station. I disembarked and walked the rather long and convoluted route to the city centre. The place was busy – it was the height of the tourist season. There were two sets of buskers attempting to outplay each other near the entrance to a large shopping centre and the market was buzzing with people buying hot dogs, chips and burgers. The smells mingled together in a pungent and highly delicious aroma which started me thinking about food.

I queued at a stall selling a wide array of hot temptations and walked away with a jacket spud, filled with melted butter, cheese and baked beans. I sat on a nearby bench and struggled to get the flimsy plastic knife and fork to perform their allotted duty. It was a hard-fought battle which I eventually won, though not without injury. I gulped down the few swigs of lukewarm tea from the Styrofoam cup it came in, threw the containers in an already over-full bin buzzing with wasps and made my way casually toward the docks.

I was supposed to meet Jack Glaze outside the main shipping Control Office at 2pm and he was already waiting outside when I arrived at 2.15.

"Oh, you made it then Michael? – I was just about to send out a search party"

"That's original" I reposted. We shook hands while pretending to give each other hard stares. We switched to real smiles and told each other how nice it was to see each other again after all this time and how we hoped we were all fine and dandy.

Once that performance was over, I followed Glaze between two metal framed buildings and into a car park situated at the back.

"In here" barked Glaze. We entered a large rundown shed which had pulleys, winches, ropes and chains dangling from the ceiling and big marine engines standing forlorn along one side.

"I like what you've done with the place Jim" I quipped. He grimaced but said nothing. We carried on, past some more ship-related gubbins, arrayed on low metal tables and ducked through a low doorway into a hot metal-walled enclosure which stank of diesel oil and grease.

There were two men inside, standing around idle, looking bored. I didn't recognise either of them. Glaze introduced them as Einar Solberg and Glen Mackie. It didn't take much skill on my part to guess which was which – one looked like a Viking and the other was a wee ginger item. Stereotypes are sometimes spot on!

It turned out this time they weren't. 'The Little Scotsman' turned out to be Einar the Norwegian and the big guy was a caber-tossing Jock from Aberdeen. I shook hands with them after I had been introduced as 'Michael Garvie – a 'new' member of the team'. Jack Glaze could be a prize ponce at times – despite his tough looks and abrasive manner.

Once the niceties had been completed, we all sat on the wooden stools provided and Glaze began droning on. I was a bad pupil and no more attentive now than I had been at school. I just couldn't stand being' lectured' – even if it was 'for my benefit'.

The gist of the speech was that I was to go off with my two new best friends, collect a fancy boat of some sort and rendezvous with some obscure associates where we would be enlightened further. These secret service Johnnies sure liked to act mysterious.

"Ok, so where are we going – if it's not top-secret Jack?" I enquired.

"Norway".

Chapter 4

Henningsvær is a fishing village in Vågan Municipality in Nordland County, Norway. Population approximately 500 people. It is located on several small islands off the southern coast of the larger Austvågøya island in the Lofoten archipelago. The village, located about 20 kilometres southwest of the town of Svolvær, is mostly located on the islands of Heimøya and Hellandsøya and connected to the rest of Vågan via two long box girder cantilever bridges made of prestressed concrete. The Engøysundet Bridge is the northern bridge and it is 194 metres long with a main span of 122 metres. The Henningsvær Bridge is further south and is 257 metres long with a main span of 150 metres.

In other words, it's not so much the middle of nowhere as the very outer edge of nowhere. It is over 100 miles north of the Artic Circle. If you like cold isolation, it's definitely the place to go.

On the plus side, the scenery is exceedingly beautiful and the air is so clean that your lungs have to become acclimatised to the lack of toxins – a bit like giving up smoking. It is peaceful, with a few small lodges and hotels for backpackers and adventurous tourists during the part of the year when there is any light and the water temporarily thaws out for a couple of months.

At least we were here in the 'hot' season – if you call 15 degrees centigrade hot. We also had light all day and most of the night too, so we were definitely seeing Henningsvær at its best.

The scenery was a breath-taking mix of snow-covered mountains and crystal-clear waters – perfect for climbers and divers alike.

The flight in a twin-engine jet from a tiny run-down airfield just outside Acle took 5 hours to reach the slightly larger airport of Svolvær. Less than an hour later we pulled up in Henningsvær Harbour in a Land Rover which had been waiting for us when we disembarked the aircraft.

The whole operation had been slick and highly discreet. There were no check-ins or customs – it was obviously being managed at a high level.

Glaze, Mackie, Solberg and I clambered out of the vehicle, which drove off. We stood on the concrete harbour-side looking around us, gathering information, surveying our environment. We had been provided with rucksacks which, according to the little blond guy who had driven us here in the now departed Land Rover, contained 'everything we needed' – which sounded highly unlikely to me.

"Right, let's get onboard" It was Glaze who spoke. I had no idea what he meant by this and by the look of Solberg, neither did he.

I picked up my bag and followed Mackie along the side of the harbour to where a fishing boat stood alongside the harbour wall. The large boat had the number ST-39-P on the side but no name. The upper decks were a pristine white – the keel was a very bright red.

We climbed a metal ladder and walked across the main deck to a steep set of steps which took us into the cabin below. It was surprisingly spacious and nicely furnished – like a luxury hotel suite, with comfortable

15

armchairs, a wide sofa and a small dining table at the far end. There was even a television in the corner.

"This is nicer than my house" quipped Solberg, plonking himself down in one of the chairs. "Very comfortable"

"Don't get too cosy Einar" replied Glaze – "there's a briefing in twenty minutes – Otto will show you to your cabins".

I was about to ask who the fuck Otto was, when a tall thin man wearing a white sailor suit moved in from the doorway at the front of the salon – there was a wooden panelled corridor with doors leading off both sides. He was either the captain of this tub or a man with 'dressing up issues.' I was relieved when he introduced himself as Captain Otto Larsson.

We followed him into the corridor and were allocated a cabin each. Mine was on the starboard side. Through the porthole I could see the hotels and shops which lined the harbour. I threw my rucksack on the table next to my bed and unzipped it.

Inside were various rolled up items of clothing – all black – including a balaclava and some uncomfortable-looking army boots. There was also a dagger, two guns and lots of ammunition. My rucksack had obviously gotten mixed up with the luggage of a member of the S.A.S.

I opened the small wardrobe which was built into the corner of my cabin and found a lot more military and 'Special Ops' type clothing and hardware – including what looked to me like some small bombs.

"Come through to the main cabin and I will explain everything" It was Glaze who spoke – he had been standing there smiling to himself as he observed my expression as I opened my cupboard.

"I was hoping there'd be a nice comfy pair of slippers and a fluffy dressing gown in here" I said.

"It's not exactly that kind of mission Michael" he replied.

"Yeah, I'm beginning to realise that Jack". I closed the wardrobe and followed him back into the main cabin, where somebody had set up a projector and screen. Everybody else was already there – sitting all over the nice soft furnishings in front of the screen. I found a piece of sofa next to the giant Mackie and took a deep breath. This could prove interesting.

Chapter 5

The projector began to roll. A black and white image appeared on the screen. It was a shot of ex-detective sergeant Harries – the man who had kidnapped my sister and her two sons – and who had forced me at gunpoint to help him try to escape. Fortunately for me – though not for him, the attempt had failed and my family had been released. He was now serving two life sentences for murdering one police officer and seriously injuring another.

"As some of you may know, this man was a sergeant in the Flying Squad and also a mole for the crime syndicate we are here to discuss."

This was news to me – I had no idea what we were here to discuss and again the small ginger Norwegian Solberg looked as baffled as I was as to the nature of our mission. Mackie on the other hand – the big Viking-like Scot didn't react – so maybe he was higher up the food chain than either Einar or me. I couldn't imagine anyone being lower – I was told only what it was deemed necessary for me to know. Obviously, Jack Glaze – formerly Detective Inspector of Special Branch – and now an undisclosed rank in a sub-section of the British Secret Service known as G10 – knew what we were here for. It looked like Mackie did too. I was looking forward to finding out – though I was growing apprehensive now that the cat was about to be released from the bag. My experience of dealing with Glaze had taught me that he tended to be involved in highly charged situations and was a tough customer. This was not going to be a picnic.

"Since receiving his prison sentence, Mr. Harries has become considerably more talkative. He has in fact furnished us with a lot of useful information regarding the drug smuggling operation we had been investigating when we first became aware of his un-policeman-like tendencies towards murder and kidnap." Glaze clicked a button on the projector and a photograph of my nemesis, Mark Hopkins flicked into view.

"Fucking Hell, not him again!" I couldn't help myself – the thought that Hopkins could have any bearing on my present situation was highly depressing to me. He had caused me to get caught up in some very unpleasant situations and was still potentially a threat to my existence.

"If I could just have a bit of silence there at the back" Glaze quipped, an amused smirk on his face.

"Sorry Jack" I replied.

"Mark Hopkins is currently in the custody of the French police and is being transported to a safe house in Paris. We have strong evidence that there is an open contract out on him and the likelihood of his imminent demise is extremely high."

"Good"

"Put a sock in it Mr. Garvie"

"Sorry".

"Hopkins is going to be moved onto a ship docked in Saint-Malo, sometime in the next 48 hours. Our first task is to rendezvous with that ship in the North Sea – five miles off the coast of Kristiansand in the south of Norway and take possession of Mr. Hopkins. Further information will be made available to you once that goal has been achieved.

"You're fucking kidding me!" I stood up and waved my arms around in frustration. "What is this, some sort of a joke?" Glaze came over and put his hands on my shoulders.

"Michael, this has all been extensively planned and you are not in possession of the entire picture. Just go along with it and you will find the situation is fully under our control".

"It's not fully under *my* control – so obviously I'm not included in the 'our' of which you speak."

"Things have moved on a lot since you had dealings with Mr. Hopkins. He is no longer a threat to you".

"Does he know that?"

"Yes, he does". I was once again being kept in the dark and given only minimal information. The same marginal level of information I had received from Mark Hopkins himself when I had been tangled up in his web of crime and deceit. I had for some reason expected a more relaxed approach now I was linked up with the 'Good Guys' – but no, it was the same old mushroom treatment.

"I'll have to take your word for that Glaze" I barked.

"Yes, you will" he growled.

I seethed during the next half hour or so of Glaze's briefing which consisted mainly of details regarding the ship, sailing times, radio silence, call signs and weapons guidance. All very interesting probably. I just kept thinking about the fact that a man who had tried to kill me and who had murdered two people I knew and attempted to frame me for their killings was now going to be brought onto this boat in the middle of the North

Sea. It seemed wrong. I couldn't understand – and as usual I was not informed as to why it was happening.

I was in the dark concerning my presence here at all. After the court case against Harries, I had been left alone by the 'powers that be' for over a year – until one morning I had been summoned to Inspector Glaze's office in Whitehall – except he wasn't 'Inspector' Glaze any longer – he was 'Mr. Glaze' with no specific role, department or title. He was running G10 – a shadowy organisation purportedly linked to M.I.6. – though I had no way of verifying this.

Now that I was far from home, about to put out to sea with some tough-looking men I didn't know, under the command of a man who's position and identity were extremely vague, I began to wonder if this wasn't in fact some sort of elaborate fiction, designed to get me into Mark Hopkins' lethal clutches.

The story I had been sold by Glaze in his office was that Harries had given them enough information to locate and arrest Hopkins – as well as some even more useful details which I 'did not need to know at present'.

This information had enabled G10 to get a much clearer picture regarding the international drug cartel in which I had become involved when I began smuggling what I thought were containers of contraband cigarettes across the English Channel for Mark Hopkins. It turned out that these goods included hard drugs and I had been lucky to escape serious charges concerning my criminal activities.

I had lived a quiet life since this time, my only concern being the possibility of Mark Hopkins either coming to silence me himself – which he had attempted before on more than one occasion – or sending a barrage of hired assassins to do the job for him.

It had been suggested by the forces of law and order that I move well away from all of my known haunts and keep a low profile until Hopkins had been apprehended. I took their advice and moved to Norfolk where I had been living happily for several years now – until I got the news of Hopkins' detention in France and received the signal to begin this 'operation', of which I had until now received the most basic outline.

The last thing I had expected was to be brought face to face with my nemesis by the very people who were allegedly protecting me from him.

Chapter 6

We set out early next morning and were quickly sailing international waters as we moved south towards our rendezvous point off Kristiansand. Otto was the only actual crewman aboard – the rest of us 'guests' just sat about looking out to sea, 'keeping our own council' as the saying goes. The sea was placid and the journey uneventful.

We weighed anchor at a point a few miles off Kristiansand which was outside Norwegian control. We ate a basic herring-based meal, thrown together by Captain Otto, washed down with bottled water. There was not much chat and no banter. Not a good sign in my experience. In fact, the level of tension in the atmosphere had been subtly but consistently rising since we left Henningsvær.

My reasons for becoming tense were obvious – I was about to come face to face with a powerful enemy. I didn't understand why the rest of my associates were getting stressed. That they knew something I didn't, was obvious but what that was and why it was causing such a strain on my shipmates I couldn't begin to guess.

"The boat is ten minutes away" stated Otto, after having spoken to the skipper of the other craft on the ship's radio. If I hadn't given up smoking, I would have lit one up about now. Instead, I let out a sigh which just put everyone else on edge. Fuck 'em.

I went onto the upper deck and peered out to sea. Nothing on the starboard side – or port either. I went astern and there was a massive oil tanker closing in rapidly. It was not what I had expected at all.

23

Otto manoeuvred our craft to enable the larger vessel to settle close enough but not too close. A small motor launch was being lowered from the tanker with two men in it. As it got nearer, I could make out the features of the men. One was a smartly dressed sailor in a grey uniform – I did not recognise the garb, though it had a military look to it. The second man – the one not piloting the boat – was Mark Hopkins.

He was wearing a smart charcoal grey single-breasted suit and looked clean and fresh – in fact he looked like a new man – his hair was tidy; he was clean shaven and there was a twinkle in his eye. It looked like French life had worked wonders for him.

He climbed aboard the Red Boat and stood on the deck, facing me.

"How's tricks, Squirrel?" his voice was full of friendly bonhomie. I walked forward, covering the twenty paces in seconds and landed a vicious right hook on the left side of his jaw. He fell to the floor. I managed to get a couple of nasty kicks into his ribs before Otto and Mackie could drag me off him.

"I'm very well, Mark, thanks for asking – and how are you on this bright sunny day?"

Hopkins got up and brushed his nice suit down, but it was now creased and some boat muck stuck to the left leg of his previously well-ironed trousers. He rubbed his jaw and stretched to re-settle his ribs. He grimaced as he did so. I awarded myself a couple of points.

"I guess I owed you that" Mark moved towards me. The friendly look still on his face.

"Oh, that's just a down payment Hopkins – there's plenty more coming your way pal" I was shocked by the level of sheer hatred in my voice. I had been carrying a lot of resentment towards this man for many years and the release was like a tidal wave. Captain Otto and Glen Mackie kept a tight grip on my arms. I attempted to pull free but they were stronger than I was.

"If you promise to behave yourself, we'll let you go" drawled Mackie.

"Alright, I will control myself" I replied. They released my arms. I fought down a massive urge to go for Hopkins again but somehow overcame it.

"Let's all go below and have a drink" suggested Otto. He began walking towards the steps. Mackie indicated that I should go next, so I did, with Big Glen behind me and Hopkins following along behind. As I turned, I noticed a half-smirk on Mark's face which made me want to smash him again but I kept on walking.

Glaze was waiting next to the drink's cabinet. "Ok, what's your poison gentlemen" He spoke like he was giving a speech in a business meeting. I ordered rum, as did Otto. Hopkins and Mackie both had Scotch. Glaze wasn't drinking and Einar Solberg was not present – maybe he was driving the boat. It was all very civilised.

Glaze continued in his role as Master of Ceremonies. "Gentlemen, this is a very unexpected situation and what I have to say now, may come as a great shock to at least one person here present."

"No shit!" I couldn't help piping up.

Mark Hopkins sat in one of the comfy chairs and looked calm, amused even. Glaze continued.

"The operation we are now involved in, is part of a much larger project to disrupt and destroy several major criminal elements currently plaguing Britain and her allies. There has been a lot of very important groundwork done over the past six years, by which certain operatives have

25

built extreme deep cover positions inside some of these criminal cartels. The lengths we have gone to, to enable these agents to gain integrity with these cartels has been remarkable."

I sipped my rum and wished I'd never given up smoking. There was an odd atmosphere growing which I didn't like and my neck was getting tense.

"Up until now there has been a blanket over the information concerning these operatives and the actions they have taken as we have had reason to believe that moles and surveillance agents allied with our enemies have been infiltrating some of our operations. Only a few hours ago I personally received information that there was such a mole on board this boat – despite our extreme procedures to nullify the likelihood. That mole was Einar Solberg. He is now dead and resting in Davy Jones' locker. As Mark was arriving and everyone was concentrating their attention on his boat – I noticed Solberg using a small communication device in a furtive manner. He was notifying somebody that Mark Hopkins was coming aboard and possibly giving our current coordinates. We have to assume that Mark's cover has been blown".

A wave of shock engulfed my mind – my body was tight and hot.

"What the fuck do you mean 'Mark's cover?'" I screamed. "Don't try to give me that bullshit. That bastard has killed at least two people in cold blood and framed me for both murders - he also tried and almost succeeded - in killing me himself on more than one occasion. I might be stupid but I'm not that fucking stupid!"

The wave of fury which swept over me was competing with the wave of fear coming in the opposite direction. I gulped down the rest of my rum, stood up, sat down again, punched the side of the armchair and shook my head from side to side.

"I know it's come as a big shock to you Michael" Glaze attempted to soothe my conflict. "But we have been unable to tell you anything about what was really going on until certain scenarios had played out. The reason we are here in the North Sea, isolated from all possible observers – or so we thought – is because the important chess pieces are now in position and we are going in for the kill – time to turn the tables on the bad guys"

"Apart from Solberg being a spy in our midst, of course" I wasn't even sure that what Glaze had told me about Solberg was true - maybe Glaze was a mole and he had just got rid of one of our team. The whole setup felt like a nightmare. I felt an urge to dive over the side of the boat into the water, but I probably wouldn't be able to swim to any land from our current position – there was no land to swim to. I would have to use a new strategy.

I trusted no-one on this boat and would have to play along until I could find a way of escaping their clutches. I made a half-successful attempt to pull myself together.

"Michael, if you just relax, we will put you completely in the picture. You may find a lot of it hard to believe and we cannot offer any proof of what you will hear – not at the moment – though if and when we complete this mission you will be shown the database of files relating to the entire operation and you will know everything"

"That'll make a change from knowing nothing, then" I griped.

Mark Hopkins stood up and walked to the front of the projector screen. Glaze shook his hand.

"I will let Commander Hopkins take it from here"

Chapter 7

Over the next two hours I heard a complex and unlikely tale of espionage, high level crime and military planning which was too ridiculous not to be true. The projector showed images which confirmed part of the setup which I wouldn't have believed possible if I hadn't seen them with my own eyes.

Commander Mark Hopkins of Special Forces spoke calmly and with authority. I believed every word he said. I discovered how and why I had been drawn into this operation and was at last able to clear some of the fog which had for the past five years, infected my brain. I was still in a perilous situation, surrounded by dangerous people but maybe, just maybe, I was not in any danger from them – they could be on my side. Dammit, it only made sense if it were true – the intricate activities described could not have been fabricated if it were not accurate – there would be no reason to create it – it would be absurd.

Everything, from the phone call I got from Johnny Walsh, his murder and my being framed for it – the killing of Art Mercer; Harries; the kidnap of my sister and her two kids – fitted in to what I was being told. It had to be authentic.

All those years ago, when Johnny Walsh had phoned me and asked me if I would collect some engine parts from Art Mercer for him, I had been part of a plan. Johnny Walsh had an ulterior motive for getting me to collect those 'parts' for him. He was blackmailing Art Mercer and I was the mug chosen to collect the pay-off.

The package I was supposed to collect was not engine parts but £10,000 in cash. The first instalment from a nice little racket Johnny thought he had going, after he discovered that Art Mercer was part of a big drugs cartel, shipping heroin and cocaine into Britain via the English Channel.

Johnny never got his pay-out. Art Mercer blew his head off with a shotgun and then hid the murder weapon in my van when I fortuitously turned up at Johnny's place to get the petrol money, he had promised me. Art couldn't resist leaving the cops a red herring – I was just in the wrong place at the wrong time.

When Art Mercer's drug bosses found out about this, they decided to eliminate Art in an attempt to close off any leads to them. He had become a weak link – if Johnny had found out what he was up to, then maybe he had been careless enough to leave other clues to his behaviour. The person they chose to eliminate the risk of Art Mercer was undercover operative Mark Hopkins who carried out the task.

The Secret Services had been watching me all along – even before I went on the run. I had been involved in small scale contraband smuggling with Mark Hopkins – no doubt chosen because of my links to Johnny Walsh – and my acquaintance with Art Mercer. They felt I might be useful at some point. And so it proved.

After the bosses had ordered the killing of Art Mercer and given the job to Mark, he watched and waited until such time as I decided to contact Art Mercer to glean information from him as to who had killed Johnny and why. I never really expected Art to know but I had to talk to anyone who knew Johnny and who might have known why he had been murdered and what he had been involved in.

I had been tracked all the way to Art's workshop and Mark Hopkins – in order to help deepen his cover, rather than blow it by refusing the job - nipped in ten minutes before I arrived, blasted Art with a shotgun, switched the weapon for another which was empty and had not been fired and made sure I got my finger prints all over it when he passed it to me to prove it had not been fired.

He then wrapped it in some yellow tarpaulin and told me he would dispose of it. At some point he fired this gun and made sure the police got it - making me the prime suspect in a second brutal slaying.

From then on, I was in Mark's power and would be a controllable asset to be used as required. Or so he thought. When I had slipped Mark's clutches – on more than one occasion, the drug lords had decreed me a liability and Mark was given the task of 'taking care of me' in the same way as he had disposed of Art Mercer.

Mark did not want to kill me if he didn't have to. I was small fry and relatively innocent unlike Art who had been knowingly involved in major drug smuggling and had murdered Johnny Walsh.

Hopkins decided to have me abducted in the English Channel and taken to France where I could be kept out of the way safely. He would then inform the drug bosses that I had been got rid of and his cover would be even stronger. Unfortunately for Mark, he used a couple of amateurs to grab me and I escaped their clutches.

This was when he decided to take control of the situation himself – he was not willing to blow his cover –

and the entire Secret Service operation - just to save my skin – he would finish me off himself before it became known that I was not dead. It was not a job he relished but he had to protect his hard-earned deep cover at all costs.

G10 was licenced to kill and operated well outside any law. This was a sub-department of the British Secret Service that the Prime Minister didn't even know about. Their remit was to 'Infiltrate and Eliminate'. They would get inside criminal and terrorist organisations and move up as high as they could, before killing as many of the members of that organisation as possible. No arrests, no court cases – just dead bad people. Occasionally they had to kill or disappear people who were less bad – or even good people if there was an imminent risk of their cover being blown. I became one of these imminent risks. Which is why Mark Hopkins had tried to blow me up in my boat and then rammed my boat, smashing it to smithereens when that didn't work.

As things panned out, Mark Hopkins managed to keep his deep cover intact – mainly by acting like a maverick intent on killing anyone who crossed his path.

He 'escaped' to France, where he stayed beneath the official 'radar'. In fact, he had been in contact with G10 *and* the drug cartel during this period.

There had been murmurings within the criminal organisation about him having become a liability – some even suggested a mole. Others took his extreme violence as a sign of his trustworthiness, believing it unlikely that an undercover agent would go to such great lengths to protect his true identity. No firm decision had been made, though the crime bosses were happy to let him stay out of the picture.

Once the news of his arrest in France became known, things changed. He was now an imminent risk to those above him and an 'open' contract was put out on him. This meant that anybody could attempt to kill him and whoever succeeded would receive the pay-out which was rumoured to be one million American Dollars.

G10 knew that Mark's cover, if not blown, was now compromised – even if he was not suspected as a mole, he was definitely seen as a high risk to the cartel and it became top priority to have him taken out of the picture.

The new G10 plan was for it to become known that Mark Hopkins was in fact a Secret Service undercover operative. This would set the entire world of organised crime alight and he would become the most hunted man on the planet.

If what Glaze had told us about Einar Solberg being a spy in our midst was true, then it was highly likely that the drug lords not only knew that he was a British agent but also knew exactly where he was.

I had a deep suspicion that Solberg had been brought onto the Red Boat specifically so he could alert the crime syndicate of the facts regarding Mark Hopkins true identity and our current location. Once he had communicated with his bosses, he was of no further use to G10 and Glaze had disposed of him by killing him and throwing him overboard. The elaborate travel plans and 'secret' rendezvous with the oil tanker from which Hopkins had been 'smuggled' had all been a ruse to convince Solberg that it was a genuine attempt to avoid detection by the cartel, whereas in fact it was nothing of the sort.

There was no doubt that I was in the company of ruthless people and only had their word for it that I was not still being used as some kind of pawn in their very complex high stakes game. No change there then.

Chapter 8

We had a meal, consisting mainly of herrings, prepared by Captain Otto, drank a couple of beers each and set off in the direction of England – Dover to be exact.

I got a very strong feeling of déjà vu as we approached the straits of Dover – it was five years since I had gotten tangled up in this mess and being back in the same vicinity – especially with Mark Hopkins and Glaze on board – made me shiver with a sense of dread.

As we moved into the harbour I looked up to my left where the White Cliffs pub still sat on its hill, brooding and taunting me. I had managed to repress a lot of the feeling I felt while on the run and seemingly tied by some invisible evil string to the pub but now these horrible emotions welled up inside me and made me feel scared and nauseous.

I went below and poured myself a Captain Morgan's Spiced Rum which I drank straight. There was a packet of Embassy No.1 cigarettes and a lighter on the table – I lit one up and felt relief flooding my bloodstream. I slipped the packet and its accompanying box of matches into my jacket pocket.

"Help yourself Squirrel, I've got plenty more". I turned and saw Mark Hopkins standing in the doorway which led to the cabins and galley.

"Thanks, I will" I snarled. I poured another two fingers of rum into my glass and sat in a chair, facing Hopkins. He leaned against the door frame and observed me like an eagle watching a mouse.

"It's a shame my cover is no longer intact" he said – his voice calm, too calm for my liking. I hate it when I feel stressed and other people feel relaxed – it's unsettling. "Still, at least everybody knows who everybody else is now – so we can cut out the subterfuge crap and get on with the annihilation phase" He couldn't help chuckling to himself as he saw me react to his words with a grimace. He walked over to the drink's cabinet, poured himself a scotch, added three rocks and sat down on the sofa, facing me.

"I'm glad you find the situation so entertaining Mark – but I suppose you have been trained for it – not to mention tons of backup, access to information and the legal authority to act in any way you choose – it must be nice"

"Whereas you, my friend, have been hunted, kept in the dark, conned, framed and nearly killed without any idea of what was going on, who was behind it or why it was happening". I gave him the hardest look I could muster at short notice.

"Mainly by you" I spat.

"You have been a pawn, a toy, a plaything"

"A MUG!!" I shouted. I would have liked to have played it cool but my long-held resentments, anger and fear was spring loaded and I was not able to resist.

Mark held out his hands towards me "I understand Michael. I have caused you a lot of problems and pain – but if there's one thing you have NOT been it's a mug." I was taken aback at this and stared at him silently.

"How do you work that out?" I enquired.

"Given the fact that you were thrown into a highly stressful and dangerous situation where pretty much all

36

the odds were against you and all others involved were in possession of far superior information about what was going on – you have acted in ways that are quite frankly, highly impressive"

"Not more bullshit Mark. Please, I couldn't stand any more of it" I slumped into my chair and took a couple of long drags of my cigarette.

"No bullshit Michael, not this time. You started out as a mug, that's true, but your survival instinct and decision-making abilities were second to none. In fact, I was so impressed I wanted you brought in on this mission." He got up, refilled his glass and sat down again. "You escaped from me more times than I would have thought possible – you survived murder attempts, abductions, evaded capture from the entire British police force and outsmarted me personally on more than one occasion – a thing which I can assure you almost never happens"

"Don't mention it" I quipped. I felt a bit of my natural Smart Arse beginning to reassert himself. What Mark said was true – irrespective of his reason for saying it – facts is facts as they say. I had survived when the odds were completely against me.

"Also, I'd like to apologise to you personally for the trouble I have caused you Michael – it might sound unbelievable given all that happened but it was never personal"

"I'd call trying to kill me pretty damned personal Mark"

"I take your point. Unfortunately, it is part of G10's remit to do whatever it takes – even if it is against our natural instincts or the law – to destroy as many high-level criminals as possible – by any means necessary. We take enormous risks and are in constant danger. The public may be outraged if they knew some of the things we do but they are safer, much safer because of it."

"Stop. You'll have me in tears"

"Fair enough".

I shifted in my chair. I wasn't comfortable with this heart-to-heart kind of talk.

"It was the kidnap of my sister which really pissed me off. Why drag innocent people into it?"

"Who is truly innocent?" Mark smirked. Then realising I was losing my temper at his blasé attitude towards my loved ones he straightened up. "Sorry, Squirrel, just ignore that comment". He sipped his drink. "Your family were not supposed to be taken at all. Harries was supposed to be keeping an eye on them until I gave him the all-clear that you had been eliminated and the drugs were safely back in England and hidden in a secret location. He was then supposed to just go back to his office in the Flying Squad and carry on being our mole there"

"So, what happened?"

"Leo Thomas happened. After he rescued you from the English Channel he got a message through to Harries – his nephew – that you were still alive and that I was still at large. You had crucial evidence against me and I had crucial evidence against both Harries and Thomas".

"I see" was all I had to offer – I was finding it fascinating – to finally understand why the things that had happened to me had transpired, made it all feel a lot less crazy – I had relished the feeling of 'normal' since falling into a maelstrom of confusion when this business had begun.

"Harries freaked out at this point and took your family hostage at Uncle Leo's house – shooting two coppers in the process. He knew that if you talked and I was arrested before he could escape, then it was highly likely that I would tell what I knew about him and Leo and the whole house of cards would fall. Harries and Leo – once they became a danger to the cartel – would also get contracts out on them – the lad just flipped – I suppose that's what you get when you try to get a boy to do a man's job."

"I guess it makes sense when all the facts are known". I lit up another of the cigarettes I had stolen from Mark – offering him one which he took with a wry smile.

"Thanks, that's very generous of you"

"Don't mention it Mark" I replied while lighting both cigarettes with Mark's matches.

"As you probably know from what Glaze has told you, Harries decided to start singing like a canary after he got a double life sentence. Seems he didn't like paying such a big price to save the arses of people who didn't lift much of a finger to help him after he got busted".

"That's understandable. Did he tell you anything you didn't already know?" I enquired.

"Plenty"

Chapter 9

Captain Otto moored the Red Boat at the far end of the harbour at Dover and killed the engines. It was mid-afternoon and our plan was to start ruffling a few feathers as soon as it got dark.

Our first target was Leo Thomas – we would be making a surprise visit to his nice big house – 'Fleetwood'; the place where my sister and her two sons had been held hostage by Liam Harries and which had been unsuccessfully searched for the drug stash.

Because we worked outside the law, we had much more opportunity to really put the frighteners on the elusive Mr. Thomas – he could shove his fancy lawyers up his shiny arse as far as G10 was concerned. We could put him in actual danger – not just threaten. Damn it! We could shoot the bastard if we felt like it.

At 10.30 pm a large black van pulled up, driven by a big man wearing black clothes and a balaclava. He spoke to no-one, just parked by the harbour and waited for us to get in the back of the vehicle. Then he put the van in gear and we moved off. SAS?

When we got to Uncle Leo's pad it was quiet. We waited at the bottom of the driveway until most of the lights had gone off and it seemed likely that Leo and his family were in bed.

We filtered in quietly and the guy in black had the front door open in seconds. No alarms went off.

We each pulled out a weapon of some sort – I had a small pistol which I had been 'issued' just before we arrived at Dover harbour. I had not had to sign for it – G10 preferred not to use paperwork as it had a habit of becoming 'evidence'. Mark Hopkins carried a sawn-off shotgun – he had experience with them – Mackie had some sort of machine gun.

The guy in black lead the way upstairs and straight into Leo Thomas' bedroom where he lay half asleep next to his voluptuously blonde wife – Gigi – half his age.

"Good evening, Leo" Mark Hopkins voice was full of menace.

"Who is that?" asked Leo – fumbling to switch on his bedside light. He flinched visibly as he saw who was standing in front of him, holding a gun. "Mark – what the hell is going on?"

"You might well ask" replied Mark, cryptically. There was a flurry of movement to the side as the possible SAS man moved round to Gigi's side of the bed and had a piece of tape over her mouth before she could even scream. Two seconds later a metallic click indicated that he had handcuffed her hands behind her back.

"Time to start spilling the beans Leo". Glaze stepped forward from out of the shadows. Thomas recognised him from the court case in which his nephew Harries had been convicted.

"Inspector – what the heck is happening – you have no right"-

"Sorry to contradict you Mr. Thomas but it is you who have no rights – none whatsoever!" Glaze barked. "You have in fact only five minutes to live!"

"Who are you – what's"

"Stop burbling and blustering Leo – this is the moment of truth – and you only get one chance to come out of it in one piece" Leo somehow pulled himself together and sat still on the bed.

"OK, what is it you want from me?" he asked.

"Everything" Glaze replied.

"First of all, we want the name of your top contact in the drug gang – and you have five seconds to answer" Mark Hopkins' voice was laced with threat and dripping with venom. Thomas squirmed.

"Look guys, you're making a big mistake here I assure you" He screeched in horror as Hopkins pulled a trigger and Gigi's head exploded in a tsunami of red, stringy gore – much of it splattering Leo's horrified face.

"Oops" Hopkins did a comedy shrug and pointed the shotgun directly at Leo Thomas.

I just about managed not to freak out or scream. I was appalled at what Hopkins had done but knew I would not be able to make any difference to how this scenario played out. My heart thumped in my chest; I could feel the blood pounding in my ears. My legs had gone to jelly.

"Five seconds" repeated Hopkins.

"Jerry Trent – it's Jerry Trent!" screamed Leo Thomas – all his former confidence gone now that he faced the reality of violence directed at himself. He had always enjoyed violence towards others but this wasn't quite such a great laugh. He would need more than a fancy lawyer to get out of this in one piece.

"And who the fuck might Jerry Trent be?" it was Mackie who spoke – he waved his machine gun around as he moved closer to the petrified thing which had once been a big shot in the local boating community and a major drug importer to the United Kingdom.

"Jerry Trent is the guy who arranges the stuff to come in from France – like a wholesaler – he's linked to the American bosses – you know – the Cartel"

"So, you order the stuff from Trent and he sends it over the Channel from France, then, does he?" asked Hopkins. I would be surprised if Mark did not already know that as he had been involved in this trade himself at quite a deep level. Interrogators often began with questions they knew the answers to in order to find out if the person being questioned was telling the truth or not.

"Not exactly – it works the other way round – the Cartel bosses decide how much we have to buy from them each month – Trent usually calls me up about a week before the shipment is sent and informs me how much of the stuff I have to buy and at what price – it's not exactly free trade"

"Ok Leo, that's better – now where does the stuff originate?"

"I don't know where it's made – if that's what you mean - Middle East maybe – it ships out of France via St. Malo – but Mark would know more about that end of things than I would" Uncle Leo was getting some of his courage back – maybe he still thought of Hopkins as some sort of underling who had gotten out of his pram and needed putting back in his place.

Hopkins laughed to himself in a way which made my flesh crawl – he could be incredibly menacing when he wanted to be - which was most of the time. Thomas shrank visibly at this – it didn't bode well for him.

"How does Trent contact you?" Glaze spoke calmly – he was not perturbed by what had happened so far.

"He phones me on my home number – just asks for a Mr. Jones – I say 'wrong number' he says something like 'I'm sorry I thought this was 100-2550 – which would mean 100 kilos at two thousand five hundred and fifty pounds per kilo - £25,500 in total"

"And is it always the same amount – 100 kilos?"

"No, it varies a lot – it can be as much as 1000 kilos – which is too big for me really – but they are not people you want to cross so I have to pay up – usually the price per kilo on these big shipments is lower – sometimes only a grand per kilo – I just have to stash it until we can get it out onto the streets"

"Do you have a way of contacting Trent – say in an emergency?" Glaze was enjoying doing a bit of questioning again – it reminded him of his days in Special Branch.

It looked to me as if Leo Thomas was toying with the idea of lying to us at this point but Hopkins waved his shotgun and Leo crumbled.

"I have a number – and an address – but it's probably just a staging point – not his home contact details"

"You let us worry about that Leo – just give us the details".

Leo gave us the details. In return, Hopkins blew his head off.

Chapter 10

Back on the Red Boat, we set out to sea in double quick time, Otto steering a course which fed us into the too familiar Channel and towards the French coast. Seven hours later we were passing the beautiful island of St. Anne and turning due south towards Jersey.

There had not been much discussion or comment regarding what had occurred last night inside the big house called Fleetwood, in which Leo Thomas had finally met up with the consequences of many years of criminal activity. He had thought of himself as a big shot – but now he was just shot. He had hidden behind lawyers and people he had bought off and had enjoyed the money he made from the misery he had inflicted on others. Now there was one less bad guy in the world – and I felt strangely elated at the thought that evil could be nullified so easily and permanently if governments only had the stomach for this sort of direct action.

Out next major target was an American named Jerry Trent – based in St. Malo. France. Mark Hopkins was already aware of him – had in fact met him more than once while working in deep cover disguised as a drug gang member. The questioning of Thomas had simply been a way of verifying what Hopkins – and Glaze – already knew. If Thomas had given other names – these might have been lies – or other unknown members of the cartel. As it turned out, no new names were forthcoming so it was Jerry Trent's turn to answer some questions.

As the powerful engines of our craft drove us through the flat seas, I discovered that our boat was a lot more than a Norwegian fishing vessel – she was equipped with radar deflectors, weapons and vast amounts of supplies, as well as top of the line telecommunications equipment. She could not be tracked.

Our mission was clear – find the next person in the food chain of the drug cartel; kill as many of them as possible. Not just the gang members and bosses, anyone and everyone even marginally linked to their evil industry – we were to wipe out the whole of the European and American drugs trade if we could. We felt sure we could do immense damage to them – it was just a matter of how good we were and how lucky.

They would not take it lying down – there was far too much money at stake – not to mention reputations. The cartel had already shown itself capable of infiltrating the highest echelons of society – including the police, Secret Service and government departments – hell, they had even got a man onto this very boat – in the shape of Einar Solberg, who Glaze had so conveniently discovered sending a message and disposed of without letting any of us know what was happening – we had only his word that this is what happened. I had a feeling of uncertainty about Glaze – I didn't like the way he had got rid of Solberg before we could question him.

To be honest I had some doubts about everyone on the boat – including myself. Why was I really here at all? – I couldn't see how I was needed – Hopkins, Glaze, Mackie and Otto seemed more than capable of dealing with any situation they were likely to encounter without me – an unprofessional petty crook and all-round mug – getting in the way. I couldn't even see that I would be any use as a fall guy – like I had been before – things had moved on to a far higher level of sophistication and nobody in their right mind would believe I was capable of operating at this level without advanced and professional help. I was way out of my depth and although I had been given a lot more information than I had before, I still did not know what they really wanted from me. I would need to stay alert.

We docked in St. Malo around noon and spent a couple of hours catching up on sleep and getting some food down our necks.

Later in the afternoon Mark Hopkins led us – all carrying holdalls with weapons in – to the hideout and main drug distribution centre for Europe. He had been in contact with the people who ran the operation for several years – from the moment he began to build his deep cover as a ruthless drug smuggler – up until he was 'arrested' by the French police whilst hiding there just a few weeks back.

The building - the cartel's main distribution warehouse on the continent - was a stronghold, guarded day and night by alert men with large guns. As we approached – led by a man they knew to be one of their own – they relaxed just enough to give us the advantage we needed. Hopkins and Mackie brought their silenced pistols into play and we were inside before anyone knew enough to start running.

Once inside a bloodbath ensued – Mackie brandished a Kalashnikov, sweeping the entire building with hot lead at a rate which none could resist – or survive.

Mark Hopkins had run up a flight of metal stairs and disappeared into an office above – I heard one shot, a scream, and then Mark came back down, dragging a terrified man by the collar.

Otto held a pistol but looked about as keen on getting involved in the slaughter as I felt. Glaze had taken a couple of pot-shots but might have been firing into empty space as far as I was concerned – our 'team' was definitely built up of two types of personality – those who seemed to relish the opportunity to kill and those who were keen to avoid it if at all possible – which got me wondering why some of us were deemed necessary on this mission at all.

Mackie sauntered back over to where we all stood – in a semi-circle facing Hopkins and his captive – the man was shaking and rambling in French – Hopkins replied to him in the same language from time to time. At one point Hopkins laughed in a mocking manner. Then he raised his pistol and shot the man through his left temple, letting him fall to the floor like a discarded puppet.

"Right, let's get back to the boat" Hopkins was definitely the one giving orders – I couldn't figure out how Glaze fitted into all this – he had originally been acting like the commander of an elite Secret Service group – but now he seemed more like a lost sheep who had wandered into a room full of hungry wolves and didn't know how to extricate himself uneaten. I was feeling the same way – but I had always been small fry, so that was to be expected.

Back on board we changed out of our 'work clothes' and after we had all showered and had a couple of shots of something alcoholic, Otto served a meal of sardines with boiled potatoes and salad leaves – which seemed rather too civilised for the recipients. I lit up one of the cigarettes I had stolen from Mark and felt a wave of relief like nothing else gave me. They may be bad for you in the long run but they certainly helped in the short term – I wasn't at all sure I would still be around in the long term so what the hell!

"De-briefing Time!" announced Glaze – he was looking more like his old self again now.

Glaze droned on for over an hour and nobody gave a shit – he liked the sound of his own voice – but the rest of us mainly drank spirits and smoked to keep ourselves awake.

The general thrust of his diatribe – if thrust be not too strong a word – was that we had 'cleared' a number of targets – in plain English he meant we had killed a lot of bad guys in cold blood to save the effort of gathering evidence and proving their guilt in court. This information was not new to us as we had all been there when it had occurred.

He went on to say that our next mission – he loved to use the word 'mission' – was to track down Jerry Trent, who – luckily for him – had not been present when we turned up at the St. Malo warehouse. This had been verified by Mark Hopkins in his French conversation with Luke Menin – the man Hopkins had heaved by the collar and questioned, before dispatching him.

According to Menin, Trent had not arrived at his expected time – he was usually very punctual. This suggested, according to Glaze – and obvious to all of us – that he had become aware of Leo Thomas' shooting and was on high alert, no doubt suspecting, quite correctly, that Thomas had given out information about him before he had been killed.

The fact that people higher up the food chain were now aware that there was a war declared upon them and that it was in fact open season, would not hinder our plans, Glaze explained – in fact it would unsettle them and possibly cause them to forget their usual caution, acting in ways which might make them more noticeable or vulnerable. We didn't care – all we had to do was cause as much outrage and alarm within their organisation as possible and execute anyone who put their head above the parapet.

We had already destroyed – or at least temporarily neutralised - their UK operation and now the whole European side was smashed in one fell swoop of bullets and blood.

It was likely that Trent – and possibly other big names in the organisation - might scuttle off back to the United States – at least temporarily – until they could cobble together a plan to counter our attack. Whatever they chose to do and however long it took them, didn't matter to us – sooner or later somebody was bound to show their hand – or their head – and we would be ready and waiting to blow it off.

After a good night's sleep, we up-anchored and the Red Boat drifted out of St. Malo, back towards the open sea.

Chapter 11

According to Glaze, we were to remain on board the Red Boat until our operation was complete – what he meant by 'complete' I couldn't begin to guess – maybe we had to kill every criminal in existence – maybe we would have to spend the rest of our lives in hiding from all the master criminals who would be searching the globe for us – forever. It was getting complex. I wished I'd not been drawn into it. Not for the first time – nor the last.

We floated about in the North Sea for a bit – living off various types of fish, incorporated into some fairly impressive dishes – Otto was a good cook – and a good boat pilot. I began to wonder if the boat belonged to him – as opposed to some nameless government department. Although basically a small and highly adapted Norwegian trawler, the Red Boat was equipped with a lot of fancy electronic equipment – not just cloaking devices and communication sets but satellite links, the latest radar and enough weapons to invade a small country. There were food stocks to last us several months and spare fuel stashed in the hold which could keep us mobile until doomsday.

When I questioned Otto about the boat and its origins, he avoided giving me any clear answers, simply explaining that he was in charge of the vessel and responsible for its day-to-day operation.

Glaze was just as cagey when I attempted to find out more about his status and role in the setup – was he in overall charge or was it' Commander' Hopkins? "Need to know basis old chap, need to know!" was all he would say.

It certainly looked to me as if Hopkins was the big dog in the show – the way he strutted and charged around the ship indicated that he was calling the shots – and nothing anyone else said or did ever contradicted my opinion on this.

Mackie, the big Scot, was a mystery – he hardly ever spoke to anyone and spent most of his time in his cabin or sitting alone beside the wheelhouse – only occasionally making small talk with Captain Otto who was usually steering or reading charts.

I sat on the deck, looking out to sea – wishing I was back in my own boat – the nice new one I had bought with the money I had received from the press a few years ago – she was called *Valerie II* and was moored back in Norfolk. I had yet to take her further than the Channel but right now I wanted more than anything to be out in the middle of the Pacific – or even further away from the unpleasant current conditions of my entangled life.

I told myself that if I ever got the chance to jump ship I would make for *Valerie II* and disappear for ever into the far reaches of a distant ocean, never to be heard of again. I would change my name and live a simple life where nobody knew me or cared to know me.

I found a huge box filled with cigarettes whilst sneaking around the hold and took possession of a carton of 200 – this should keep me going until we got back on land again. There was also a considerable amount of rum – I purloined a bottle of Captain Morgan Spiced and slunk back to my cabin to smoke and drink the day away.

We kept away from land apart from once, passing close to a small island which may or may not have been St. Anne. If we were back amongst the Channel Islands there was a chance we were heading either to France again, or staying close enough to the south coast of England to return to Dover – or Great Yarmouth. I hoped this was the case. My feet were itching to run.

The weather was mostly calm throughout this period, apart from a short-lived gale which bounced us around a bit before giving up and going back to where it came from.

Never had being on a boat been less pleasurable – we just crawled around – with no purpose other than wasting time until we received news which would again send us into action – more killing – which would appeal to Mark Hopkins – and Mackie – if to no-one else.

After two weeks – which seemed like two months – we received a radio communication from some secret part of 'Spyland'.

Jerry Trent had been located near St. Malo – unfortunately he had been arrested by the French police and taken into custody. It seems he had been grassed on by some small-time smuggler loosely involved in the French side of the operation, who had heard talk of an 'American boss'. The name 'Jerry Trent' was heard – also 'Shelton' – though the meaning or relevance of this was currently unknown.

"Well, that's pissed on our fireworks" grumbled Mark Hopkins, on receiving this information. "We can't exactly break him out of police custody – let's hope he's got a good lawyer – he should be out on bail soon enough – let's get a shift on back to St. Malo and see if we can't nab him when he comes out".

It took four hours to cross the mill pond and moor once again in the main harbour. We took a taxi to the town centre and wasted no time in locating the police station. Now it was just a case of waiting until Trent came out.

Glaze went into the police station and after flashing his credentials, managed to find out that Trent was due to be released later that evening – his solicitor was due to collect him at eight o'clock.

Our initial plan had been to abduct him when he came out and interrogate him in the back of a van we had hired locally – but Glaze decided it would be a better option to follow him – he may lead us to people higher up in the organisation without us having to resort to tactics which may or may not lead us to the prey we sought.

Promptly at eight, two men walked out of the police station and turned left. Glaze and Otto followed them on foot, while I sat in the middle of the van's bench seat, unhappily squashed between Mackie and Hopkins.

If it looked like Trent or his solicitor had spotted their trackers – we would resort to plan 'A' and bundle the pair of them into the van – it seemed likely that the lawyer would spill the beans even if Trent was too tough to squeal.

Hopkins drove slowly, keeping the men – and ours – in sight. Luckily the traffic was slow in the town centre which helped us blend in better.

Our quarry walked around the main shopping area and towards the harbour. We lost them temporarily, due to having to drive around a one-way system but Glaze kept in touch via walkie-talkie and we soon got back on their trail.

As they approached the harbour entrance, Trent began to look around to see if they had been followed – Glaze was far too experienced to be spotted however, and

54

Trent and his solicitor went inside a small office complex situated on the far side of the mooring area.

After a few minutes Glaze got back on the radio and told us he had ascertained that he could not see anyone else inside the building. He and Otto were going in.

Hopkins parked the van and opened the drivers' door. Mackie started to climb out his side.

"You stay in the van Squirrel. Keep the engine running in case we need to make a fast getaway!" As he barked the order at me, Hopkins grabbed a Kalashnikov and made his way across the tarmac, closely followed by Mackie who was toting similar hardware.

I was delighted to be left in the van. I kept my foot on the throttle and my eyes on the door they had just entered by. My dislike of the whole situation had grown to a deep loathing.

I had concluded – after seeing their method in action – that I did not like the cold-blooded killing of people – even bad people. If law and order collapsed it would be the nastiest people with the most weapons who would run the world – and if it was people like Mark Hopkins, I wouldn't want to be part of it – he enjoyed killing and was highly unpredictable.

A couple of minutes later, I heard the now familiar sound of machine gun fire – and pistol shots. A sheet of flame broke out through an exploding windowpane, followed by a loud bang.

My foot began to shake on the accelerator as I waited for my associates – I couldn't consider them 'colleagues' – to return. My nerves were in tatters – I expected a whole battalion of armed police to seal off the area any time soon and wanted to get the hell out of there.

Five minutes passed. I couldn't understand why none of them had come out – surely, they must know they had only a couple of minutes or less to get away, before they were arrested.

"Dammit" I swore as I hurriedly climbed out of the van and ran towards the building – which was now slightly on fire. I opened the door and peered inside – it was empty in the corridor. I ran towards the main office. Inside it was rather crowded – with broken bodies and dismembered limbs.

"Hopkins – are you here?" I called – no reply. I forced myself to approach the carcases and saw that Glaze was riddled with machine gun bullets – his body and part of his head oozing blood and brains all over the bodies beneath him – there was a pile of them.

Half-covered by Glaze was Mackie – also leaking from a massive hole in his skull. Slightly to the left was Otto – one leg missing – no doubt from the explosion – and brains splashed all over the place.

At the other end of the room were the bullet-riddled corpses of Trent and his legal adviser – and between the two piles was Hopkins – Mark Fucking Big Man, Master of the Universe, Mark Hopkins – laying in a pool of his own piss and blood – his body mangled by the explosion – limbs hanging by red glossy threads – eyes blank – body smashed – life gone. I was Mark's Mug no longer. I was free of him at long last. I was so relieved that I almost fell over in a faint.

I snapped out of my trance, bolted out of the building, jumped in the van and skidded out of the harbour – just seconds before a parade of police and army vehicles – lights and sirens going crazy – flashed past me in the opposite direction.

Chapter 12

I drove straight back to the boat and got on board. It was the first time I had been alone on the craft and I had never shown much interest in her. Now I needed to get better acquainted with this unusual Red Boat.

I went to the wheelhouse and had a look at the controls, which seemed fairly normal – at least as regards the driving and steering. There were a lot of extra levers and buttons which were a mystery to me but that didn't matter right now. What mattered right now was getting far out to sea as fast as possible – without drawing too much attention to myself. Once I was out in the Atlantic, I could investigate the craft's extra facilities and special operations equipment at my leisure.

I knew it was supposedly undetectable by radar and could cloak its movements and position – though I wasn't sure if this was a default setting or if it had to be switched on – it was possible that it had already been switched on by Otto – but I would like to know for sure.

There would be no problems concerning fuel or food supplies – this craft was packed to the gills with provisions and equipment – it was built to survive, stealthily and for a very long time.

It was also packed with weapons – though I had not as yet discovered the full extent of these or where some of them were hidden. I had seen enough weapons over the past few weeks to last me a lifetime – the aggression and willingness to kill shown by my former comrades had turned my stomach and I was extremely pleased to be out of their orbit once and for all.

In fact, I felt nothing but relief as I started up the Red Boat's powerful engines and piloted the craft out of St. Malo harbour – hopefully for ever. I never wanted to see the place again – or any of my recent locations for that matter – I needed to get right away from all the ties and entanglements, go somewhere with no memories. The middle of a large ocean would make a great starting point.

I headed West and moved outside the French three-mile limit. Initially I drove the boat fast – her power was amazing – but once I had passed Roscoff, I slowed to a more sedate pace and soon turned South-West until clear of Ushant. I was now in open water and moving into the Celtic Sea, heading into the wide spaces of the North Atlantic.

I slept little that night – instead enjoying a level of safety, peace and quiet I had not known for a long time. The stars shone brightly in a crystal-clear sky and the waves were small. I drank a few cans of beer and smoked a lot. Some ham sandwiches shovelled down my neck helped comfort me further and by morning I was dozing at the wheel.

I shut off the engines and was drifting around, spending the morning on the rear deck, just staring out to sea, letting my mind and emotions stabilize, when I heard the ships' radio blurt something out. I didn't catch it clearly and went down into the comms cabin to see what was going on.

There was a green light blinking, which I think meant a message had been in and was awaiting a reply. I let it blink some more. Suddenly a tinny voice started requesting that I reply – the voice said it was 'Command Control', whatever that meant.

I think what it meant was that 'they' had discovered that all their operatives had been killed and that I had taken their best toy out to sea and they wanted it back. I ignored the voice. It kept asking for confirmation of who was on board and what the boat's location was.

This was good news. It meant they didn't know where I was – the cloaking device was obviously switched on. I was pretty sure they did know who was on board though as I was the only one who had previously been here who wasn't a corpse – and they knew I had marine experience too.

I found a button with the word OFF. I pressed it and the voice went away. I felt an urge to pull all the electronic equipment out by the roots and throw it in the sea but decided it might come in useful at some point and went back up to the upper deck.

I cracked open a can of lager and sat with my feet dangling over the side, thinking about my situation and options.

One thing I was certain of was that I had had enough of all the high jinks – I wanted a place to hide – it was like the good old days again – five years ago I was a hunted man on the run from dangerous mysterious people and here I was once more in the same situation – although I now knew at least some of what was going on and who was involved. I also had a powerful, invisible boat at my disposal and I intended to make use of it to my own advantage – I was going to start playing my own game. No more crime, no more spies, no more police, no more killing. I wanted a simple life and I would damn well get it if I had to disappear into the outer reaches of the

Antarctic to get it, though I would prefer somewhere quiet and sunny.

Every other option I had would involve those G10 people, the police, and who knew what other faceless stress-inducing bureaucrats.

Chances were, they would catch up with me eventually but I was going to keep out of their way for as long as I could and I was determined to enjoy every second of my life until that happened.

I calculated that it would take me about a day and a half to reach the Azores if I set the boat's autopilot at 30 knots – as long as the weather held and nothing unexpected happened. I was expecting something unexpected to happen – but tried to block my fears out of my mind.

Once the boat's course was set, I began to study some of the vast array of electronic equipment which this specially prepared boat had installed within the wheelhouse and telecommunications cabin.

I recognised the multi-function display console mounted on the bridge infrastructure – it was far more complex than the ones I had used before but there were settings and displays for everything from depth monitoring to gyro compasses. Displays for 9-axis motion-sensors, AIS transponders and satellite communication consoles were more advanced but I was confident that given time I would be able to use of some of this high-tech gubbins to my advantage.

I was a little concerned that by switching some of it on, or adjusting settings and dials which I was usure of, that I would inadvertently alert someone to my position and direction of movement – this I definitely did not want to do.

I spent a few hours catching up on some sleep before having a leisurely shower and changing into some clean clothes. I then explored the galley and found cupboards stocked to the gills with food, drink and other necessities. I opened a tin of tomato soup, warmed it in a small saucepan on the gas burner and toasted a couple of slices of bread. A bottle of ice-cold lager from the fridge, with a cigarette and I was feeling like my old self again – or rather I was feeling like my new self.

The things I had gone through had changed me and my outlook on life – no more idle pleasures – I would from now on pursue more active pleasures – like travelling the world, seeing countries I had only heard about in books and keeping myself out of trouble as much as possible – which meant keeping out of the way of other people as much as possible. The way I was feeling, I would be quite happy if I never saw another living human – or a dead one for that matter – ever again. I was out at sea with the breeze blowing coolly across my face, and enough fuel and provisions to enable me to keep doing it for several months at least – without the need to enter a single port if I didn't want to.

The Atlantic could be a very wild place – but for me now, it was just heaven – the wind was calm, the seas had a slight bounce and the sun was warm but not too hot. Idyllic I think you'd call it.

Chapter 13

By the time I was approaching the outer edge of the Azores, the sea had become a little rougher and the Red Boat was pitching slightly. The built-in stabilising system minimised the movement though and conditions remained ideal onboard.

During my 36-hour journey from Ushant, I had time to think about what had happened and to consider my options.

Obviously, I could stay away from land and hope I would be left in peace for a long time – this had been my approach all those years ago when I had found my friend Johnny Walsh's headless corpse and had done a runner – only to find myself hunted by the police and the crime cartel. This was not a situation I really wanted to get into again.

On the other hand, I had done nothing wrong – apart from 'borrowing' a boat which I already had permission to crew on - my colleagues had all been killed but I had not broken any laws and had not killed anyone. Theoretically I was safe – my problem was I had no idea who I should contact – G10 was a secret even to most parts of Secret Service – they worked well outside the usual remit of M.I.5 and 6. It was likely that virtually no one inside the British Secret Service had even heard of them – I would have no proof that I was not part of a murderous criminal gang – after all Mark Hopkins had been on board and he had shot a lot of people.

Glaze was probably known to at least some people in Whitehall and the boat was possibly on some register somewhere. It was just a case of approaching the right people and letting them debrief me regarding the operational actions we had taken.

I made up my mind to switch the radio back on and wait until someone contacted me on it. I should be fairly safe, as the only people who would be likely to have the contact frequencies for this craft were people who were aware of the operation's existence – if not its full remit.

I went into the comms room and clicked the switch. Immediately the voice was back – asking me to reply. I picked up the handset and pressed the button on the side.

"Hearing you loud and clear Old Chap – how can I help you this fine morning?"

"Please state your current position and trajectory" the voice sounded annoyed – not surprising really as I had ignored it for a day and a half.

"I am approaching the Azores and intend to dock there in approximately two hours"

"To whom am I speaking?"

"Who wants to know?" The voice went quiet for a few seconds – possibly the person talking was conferring with someone else.

"Please moor at Ponta Delgada – we will meet you there" – They didn't seem to want to tell me who they were any more than I wanted to say who I was. I guess it was a case of neither of us choosing to give our names to someone unknown – a bit of a verbal Mexican standoff you might say.

"Roger Wilco" I signed off with my habitual Royal Air Force phrase – it amused me to use the incorrect jargon.

Ponta Delgada, on São Miguel Island, is the capital of the Portuguese Archipelago known as the Azores. As I approached, I saw the beautiful 3-arched city gates and the gothic-style Church of St. Sebastian near the harbour.

I wouldn't mind a few weeks holiday here – soaking up the sun and the Portuguese food and wines would be just what the doctor ordered. Part of me wished I had taken a few days out to sample the local nightlife and scenery before making contact with whoever it was, I had made contact with – but there was nothing I could do about it now.

The day was warming up nicely as I carefully piloted this unusual craft into a space next to the jetty and switched off the engines.

I went up onto the rear deck and looked about me. The beauty of the sun, sea and gentle surf along the beachfront was accented by the magnificence of the ancient arched gates and the even more ancient church. The houses and buildings around were colourful and the air was warm, lightened by a fresh breeze blowing in off the sea.

I cracked open a can of lager and lit up a cigarette – it was the last one in the packet I had borrowed from Mark Hopkins on board the boat. I shuddered when I remembered my last sight of his mangled and ruined corpse in the warehouse in St. Malo. Mark Hopkins had been a big part of my life for over five years and his impact had been great – mainly extremely bad. Now he was gone from my life and the world would not care one way or the other. I felt mainly relief. I had known him as a business acquaintance, a dangerous enemy and of late as a colleague on a mission for the British Secret Service.

Knowing him had been intense and often frightening and he remained a mystery to me even in death.

I sat enjoying the sun and the peace for half an hour before going below to make myself a ham sandwich. The radio had remained silent. I wondered how long I would have to wait until somebody appeared to let me know what to do next. Was my mission over? Was I still a member of G10 – if it really existed at all.

If nothing else, I knew I'd had more than enough of living like this. I wanted out – as far out as possible. Out of G10, out of England and out of reach. I pictured myself on a sunny island where nobody knew me. Then I realised I was currently on a sunny island where nobody knew me – and G10 were still linked – still close – still interested in me. Perhaps there was nowhere on Earth where their shadowy tentacles did not reach.

I went back up onto the deck and leaned against the side of the wheelhouse, smoking.

I had no idea who G10 were – I guess the whole point of secret services is to be mysterious and unclear. I would never get a clear picture – I had dealt with them long enough to know that. I would just have to move on in my life, try to push them out of my head. Part of my mind told me that G10 did not even exist – they were some bullshit cover for a criminal gang which had the resources to convince fools like me that they were the good guys – backed by stable governments – and working for the safety of the ordinary citizens who knew nothing of their existence.

The way Mark Hopkins had relished killing made it believable that he was on the wrong side – whatever side that might be. It was too much for me to deal with. I was out of my depth and needed to come ashore.

"Ahoy, Shipmate!" It was an English voice – one which sent a shiver down my spine. I turned, then staggered and almost fainted in shock. Johnny Walsh was standing on the jetty, looking up at me and smiling like a Cheshire cat.

"Johnny?" I mumbled.

"Yes Mike – it's me – good old Johnny from school" He walked towards the gangplank. "Permission to come aboard Captain?" he was thoroughly enjoying himself. I'm glad one of us was.

"What the Hell's going on Johnny?" my voice was wavering – like my mind. He took my question as permission to come on board and joined me on the deck.

"Let's get a couple of drinks down you first – you're all over the place mate". He led the way down to the main cabin and as I staggered after him, poured a couple of large glasses of Captain Morgan's Spiced. He obviously knew his way around the Red Boat.

I swigged the alcohol, spilling a little down the front of my shirt in my hurry. I sat in one of the armchairs and lit up a cigarette – the smoke combined with the rum, began to create a powerful cocktail inside my brain – adding a level of stability. I took a deep breath.

"So obviously that wasn't your headless corpse I discovered in your house five years ago then Johnny?"

"Clearly not"

"So, who was it?"

Johnny pulled a distasteful face. "That was a nasty little villain named Josh Nelson – he was about my size – just had to put him in my old overalls and boots and voilà – one dead Johnny Walsh. Hopkins took care of the killing – he tends to enjoy it"

"So, it was you who set me up from the start then?"

"Unfortunately, things didn't go exactly to plan. It all got a bit out of hand"

"A bit out of hand!!" I shouted. I suppose you could say it got a bit out of fucking hand!"

"There were other variables which did not behave as expected" by 'variables' I took him to mean people.

"Sorry to hear that" I quipped sarcastically. Johnny let it pass.

"I needed someone who knew me well to identify my body – that was the only reason you were dragged into it at all. He grimaced and shrugged. "Didn't expect you to go on the run like that – thought you'd just phone the police and tell them you had found me dead – then you could have gone home to enjoy the rest of your pointless existence in peace"

"I see now that I was one of the variables which messed up your sordid little plan. I am sorry mate" I laced my comment with a nice mix of sarcasm, resentment and venom. He ignored it and carried on.

"The problem was that Mark Hopkins took it upon himself to plant the shotgun in the back of your truck which compounded the situation".

"It ruined my day too"

"Hopkins was turning renegade – saw my disappearing act as an opportunity to make a play for top spot".

"You talk like a gangster"

Johnny chuckled. "It's a bad habit I've got into lately. Basically, Hopkins was always too ambitious for his – and anyone else's good. He was also trigger happy."

"Tell me about it"

68

"He knew most of the details and most of the people involved – thought he could take over the operation"

"What operation is that, Johnny?"

"The smuggling"

"You mean the heroin smuggling?"

"Yeah, the drugs were a lucrative trade – I had built up a big network of contacts – buyers, sellers, producers, distributors – the lot. Started out selling dope to friends of mine at discos when I first left school – remember how I always had plenty of cash when we went out on the piss?"

I did remember – he had always been fairly flush and was extremely generous to me when my meagre supply of beer vouchers ran out.

"I never knew you were selling drugs"

"You weren't supposed to know mate – didn't want to drag you into my dodgy dealings."

"Very considerate of you – how's that working out?"

"Yeah, well I didn't expect you to get mixed up in it – only needed you to identify the corpse – but you and Hopkins messed that up between you".

"I do apologise" In spite of myself I was relaxing in Johnny's company and his flippancy was not annoying me as much as it maybe should have.

"That's alright – nobody's perfect Mike"

"So, it was Hopkins who had placed the body of this Josh character in your place and I was to convince everyone that you were out of the picture?"

"That's about the size of it"

"But due to me absconding the crime scene – plus Hopkins little joke of hiding the weapon in my truck, I got into a massive manhunt situation?"

"Yep" It was good to finally get a clear understanding of why and how my nightmare had begun. If what Johnny had told me was true – and despite everything I believed him – then it all made logical sense – a part of my brain which had become fogged by the lack of understanding became clean again.

"How did Art Mercer fit into all this?"

"He was a partner of mine. When I 'disappeared' Hopkins killed him, thinking it would make the way clear for him to seize control"

"Hopkins told me Art Mercer shot you"

"Hopkins was a liar and a control freak"

So, I just happened to arrive as Mercer was killed – seems one hell of a coincidence"

"Probably Hopkins had people following you all the time – waiting until you headed out towards Art's place – it was likely you would – you had to try to find out what was going on and you knew there was a link from me to him. Hopkins got there just before you – killed Art and set you up as the fall guy – just like before"

"So why did you decide to stage your own murder, Johnny?"

"I wanted to get out of the whole business – it was getting too risky and I was starting to feel well out of my depth. He took a sip of his rum. "There were American guys trying to get a piece of the action – very big crime guys – if you know what I mean?"

"People like Jerry Trent?"

"Trent was just a middleman – mind you he was beginning to get his fingers into a lot of other people's pies. He worked for some Mafia family based in Chicago – his job was to sniff about – get a few people worried – set up a few deals to see how we operated. It would then be just a matter of time before the Yanks moved in and took over the whole operation. I decided if I was dead, I would be free and clear – I made a nice little nest-egg over the years and wanted to go into retirement".

"It makes sense when you put it like that".

"My only problem was when you got into trouble because of me – I didn't think it was right. Initially I asked Hopkins to look after you"

"He certainly attempted to 'look after me'" I couldn't help but laugh at my own joke and Johnny Walsh did too.

"Yeah, well I suppose different people have different ideas about what 'look after' and 'take care of' means"

"Mark Hopkins certainly had his own ideas" I said.

"He wanted to take over and thought his best option would be to wipe out all opposition".

"Looks like he had a damn good go at it – judging by the amount of people he eliminated since he got away from the French police"

"That was down to Glaze and G10," said Walsh. I lit up another cigarette, stretched and drank some more.

"Who exactly the fuck *are* G10 anyway? – they had me sign all kinds of secret documents and seem to be completely above the law. I suppose it's all part of the wonders of the British Secret Service"

Johnny laughed out loud.

"The British Secret Service - I love it"

"What's the joke Johnny?"

71

"I can tell you one thing for certain Mike – G10 has absolutely nothing whatsoever to do with the British Secret Service"

Chapter 14

Once it was dark, Johnny and I got the boat underway and headed off into the North Atlantic. Our plan was to head back to Henningsvær in Norway – where the Red Boat had been docked when I first went on board. Then I would just 'go home'.

It sounded simple enough but I was feeling extremely unsure if this was a good idea. Johnny assured me that the police had no reason to be interested in me now as Hopkins and most of his associates were dead – I would not need to give evidence as there would no longer be a court case.

A lot of loose ends had been 'tidied up'. The drug cartel – at least as far as I knew – was, if not wiped out, at least severely damaged – the top people in the organisation in the UK were probably dead – or would be unable to operate either through lack of manpower or due to them not wanting to be next on the kill list. The G10 operation had been highly successful. It had also been highly illegal.

G10 – at least according to Johnny Walsh, had not in actuality been any part of the British Secret Service – it had been simply an 'invention' of Johnny's to lure Hopkins and Glaze – and through them a fool named Michael Garvie – into believing they were to receive benefits of one kind or another from eliminating their former colleagues in the crime syndicate.

Hopkins was to get release from prison and a new identity as an undercover agent. Glaze – who was in fact an undercover agent of the cartel would get promotion and even more inside info regarding the workings and ongoing operations of the real Secret Service.

G10 was an invention which had taken hold. Due to the extreme 'need to know' nature of secret service dealings, it had been possible to set up a 'special operation' – G10 – inside the *real* intelligence establishment. Nobody knew the nature or remit of G10 because G10 was a 'special operation'. There were many such virtually independent cells operating inside MI5 and MI6 – G10 was not that unique.

Glaze had been recruited into Johnny's smuggling organisation some years ago – as a police constable. He had found promotion came fairly quickly if you had tip offs from certain underworld groups about the actions of rival groups. His arrest record was second to none – and Johnny Walsh had taken over a large part of the UK drug trade when his rivals found themselves in police custody.

After Hopkins had been arrested in France, he had been approached by Glaze, who in his new role as a controller in the genuine British Intelligence Services, had offered Mark a chance to turn his luck around. He would become an agent of G10 and offered the opportunity to clear away all of the people who may have incriminating evidence against him regarding his previous enterprises – and to get revenge on any of them who he considered rivals – which in Hopkins' case was pretty much everyone.

Walsh had always intended that Hopkins would come to a sticky end in the warehouse in St. Malo – the bomb which finally finished him – as well as several other gang members - had been remotely activated by Johnny Walsh himself – from a little grey car parked in the car park. The reason I had been left outside to 'keep watch' was because Walsh had instructed Glaze to make sure I didn't 'get in the way' when the shooting began – and to ensure the van was kept running and ready for a quick escape. In this way Johnny had protected me from getting killed – and to a large degree from getting involved, apart from as an observer.

I was impressed. Extremely shocked – but impressed, that my old school mate Johnny had virtually singlehandedly built up an international drug smuggling operation, got a pet copper to help him and then develop a fake undercover group within the British Intelligence community – before getting one half of the group to kill the other half – who were then in turn finished off by Johnny himself.

I also discovered something which completely twisted my understanding of another event. When Mark Hopkins had forced me to act on his behalf by telling me my sister Kirsty and her two sons had been held by his associate in the police force – I had assumed he meant Detective sergeant Liam Harries of the Flying Squad – after all, he shot two coppers and took them to the house owned by his uncle Leo Thomas. He was currently serving two life sentences in prison for these actions.

Johnny explained to me that Harries was not the police 'colleague' to whom Hopkins had referred. That had been the uniformed officer who had been shot by Harries when he escaped to his uncle's house. This officer had been given instructions to kill the hostages at a certain time of day unless he heard from Hopkins by that time. He had not heard. Hopkins had always intended that my family were killed, just as he had planned and twice attempted, to kill me that same day – once with a bomb and once by ramming my boat.

Harries had in fact volunteered to go to my sister's house in Southampton where she was supposedly under police protection, after a tip off that Hopkins had a man in there. When this man made his move Harries shot him. Unfortunately, another officer had been accidently shot in the eye in the melee. The shot had come from Harries' gun – so he had to accept prosecution for one murder and one attempted murder of police officers – even though one had been a rogue copper working for Hopkins and the other had been shot by accident during a shoot-out instigated by the rogue cop.

None of this had been mentioned in the trial – it was imperative that Harries get sent down and look like a gun-happy, possibly psychotic killer. There was now no question in the minds of the crime world that he was a 'wrong un' rather than a police double agent – a thing which he was never supposed to become but which was being used to the advantage of certain parties.

It took us four days, slow sailing to get back to the little fishing village of Henningsvær in the Lofoten archipelago of the Norwegian continent – the Red Boat's home. We moored the craft in the same position as she had been in when I first set eyes on her. We left her to do whatever boats did when nobody was watching them.

Johnny flew with me back to Oslo where I took a flight to Gatwick and Johnny waved me off after telling me he would be in touch. He assured me there should be no comeback for me regarding the recent events – I was only an observer and everyone who knew anything about the operation was dead – apart from him and I. Johnny and Mike – the old mates from school.

It was dark when I arrived back in Great Yarmouth. I had not wanted to go straight home, preferring a few hours away from my normal haunts in which to get my thoughts in order – if that were possible. I booked into a B and B on the promenade and after a much-needed shower and shave, I slept like the proverbial log.

Chapter 15

I rose early next morning and sat in the large old-fashioned dining room, wolfing down a superb Full English breakfast and several cups of strong tea. I walked outside and smoked a cigarette, breathing in the beauty of the seaside landscape along with the toxic fumes of my cigarette. It was a good combination. I felt strength – and dare I say happiness – suffuse my being.

The sea stretching – flat – as far as the eye could see. The pier extending out – filled with colourful sideshows, stalls and the call of gulls. Further to my right I could make out the log flume and roller coaster in the Pleasure Park – not open yet - and the buzz of traffic moving slowly past the beachfront hotels, restaurants and glitzy amusement arcades – based on the ones in Las Vegas but a whole lot smaller in scale and wealth.

The continual ringing of bells, tinny tunes and flashing lights from the arcades gave me a warm glow. They reminded me of sunny happy seaside days of the past when a carefree innocent boy called Mike and another called Johnny had messed about on family holidays – causing mischief and mayhem wherever they went and laughing all the time.

I shook myself out of my no doubt inaccurate reverie and walked back to my accommodation. After checking out, I walked to the railway station, bought a ticket and awaited my train back to Norwich.

The journey was pleasant - the sun shone over the wide-open grasslands of Acle and I spent my time peering out of the window at the cows, horses, small streams and ancient windmills which fill the landscape in this part of Norfolk.

The train pulled into Norwich station just before 11.30 and I was back on the road in my Land Rover before Noon.

Bloxham St. Michael was very quiet – as it always was. I drove straight to my small cottage on the River Bure and parked. I approached the door with a sense of trepidation – would there be somebody waiting inside for me? – a man with a shotgun? A police officer with handcuffs in hand? I put the key in the lock. My phone rang, startling me. I laughed at my own jumpiness and opened the front door.

"Ahoy" I answered on the fourth ring. A voice I didn't know asked me if I was Michael Garvie. I asked them who wanted to know. They said my gas bill was well overdue. I laughed and thanked them for letting me know. I told them I would get a cheque in the post. I hung up.

I put my backpack down and picked up the clump of letters and junk which had accumulated on the doormat while I had been away. Mainly bills and bullshit.

The place looked just as I had left it – apart from a layer of dust which didn't bother me in the least. I made myself a pot of strong tea and sat in my favourite armchair while I sipped it. I had my post sorted into two piles within about three minutes and placed the larger pile – the obvious junk – to one side while I opened the less obvious junk from the smaller pile. Nothing of any importance or interest – bank statements, something indecipherable from the tax office, a seed catalogue, two invoices for boat-related repair work I'd had done but not paid for yet and a new cheque book.

I began to nod off in my chair and stretched out my legs. After a short catnap, I cleared away the tea things, washed them up, filed most of the mail in the bin and the rest onto the desk in my office. I checked the fridge, which was nearly empty, apart from a nasty-looking piece of chicken which should have been thrown out before I left on my recent adventure. I put it straight into the outside dustbin and wandered around my small, picturesque garden, feeling glad to be alive and even gladder to be in my cosy little nook hidden in the depths of the Norfolk countryside. It was wonderful to be home again.

Later that afternoon I drove down to the local shop and bought a few essentials. The shopkeeper, Mrs. Bolton, was pleased to see me and after a swift and brazen interrogation as to where I'd been these last few weeks, which I fielded beautifully with glib answers, she packed up my newly purchased comestibles and wished me a cheery 'Good Day'.

I took my provisions home, before taking a short stroll along the riverside to the little boatyard. There was *Valerie II* – my pride and joy, moored at the far end of the wharf. Her white keel shining in the sun, her mooring lines creaking a little in the gentle wash of the river.

"Morning Mr. Garvie" I turned and saw Tony Smith – the owner of the boatyard and wharf – standing beside a small rowing boat which he had been painting with some sort of maritime gloop.

"Hello Tony – how's business?"

"Run off my feet" he said, laughing. It was almost a catchphrase – though completely untrue – his little joke. The yard was almost always quiet and Tony worked at a slow and steady pace borne of his ancient Norfolk roots

– he didn't hold with the modern pace of life – 'everybody in such a hurry to get nowhere' he had been heard to say on more than one occasion.

"The yard is looking good" I said

"Cleared out some of the old clutter at last" he replied. "Might be a wherry in soon and I wanted to make room in case they had need of the space." A wherry was a traditional Norfolk barge – large and often painted black with a big sail affixed. It was a beautiful craft and part of the history of county going back centuries.

"When's it due in?" I enquired.

"Should be early next week" he replied. He approached me as he spoke – wiping his hands on a filthy rag. I've kept an eye on *Valerie* – been good as gold"

"Glad to hear she's been behaving herself" I quipped. "I will bring your cheque for the mooring fees up next time I come – should be tomorrow" he waved the rag as if to dismiss my talk of business.

"There's no rush – whenever you get the time" He rested one hand on *Valerie II*'s side. "Nice boat this – are you taking her out?"

"I thought maybe a pootle into the Broads – just to get my sea legs back" Tony smiled.

"You just take it easy – it can get quite rough out there" he chortled. The broads were quiet for most of the year – apart for the massive influx of tourist boats during high summer when it could sometimes get congested with landlubbers in day-hire craft – mainly from Wroxham.

"I'll be alright – my boat's bigger than most of theirs". *Valerie II* was a Ferretti 70 – a craft with a sleek 70-foot fibreglass hull and a beam width of about 18 feet, which was equally at home in medium to heavy seas or

81

slow backwaters. Her two well-maintained MTU diesel engines were powerful enough to get her up to 28 knots or cruise comfortably at 22 knots.

I lowered the electronic gangway and went onto the spacious stern deck. The large outdoor area had teak floors and there was plenty of walkaround throughout the boat. I flopped down onto one of the sofas and rested my arms on the table. I was back in my preferred environment – I just needed to get her into some open water.

I had kept her – with Tony's help - in tip top condition and only needed to re-stock my food and drink supplies – and buy a few cartons of cigarettes – and I would be on my way.

"Diesel and water tanks full" Tony must have read my mind. "Generators tested a week ago – all fine"

"Thanks Tony – I appreciate it"

"No probs – I enjoy working on her".

I went back to my cottage and wrote out a cheque to give to Tony the following morning. I was planning to take *Valerie II* out for a spin on the broads – and who knew where else.

The rest of the day I spent sorting out a few things – writing cheques for utilities and putting them in envelopes to post tomorrow – having a shower and packing a few clean clothes and deck shoes – emptying the fridge of the fresh food I had bought that morning and eating what I could – the rest I put back in for my breakfast – mainly ham and milk. I had a couple of bottles of warm beer and a few cigarettes before falling asleep in front of the television. I finally got to bed around midnight.

I woke early and ate up the rest of the perishables. After packing my rucksack and checking that everything which had to be turned off had indeed been turned off, I went out of the front door, locking it behind me and sauntered down to the post office in the village.

Mrs Bolton was not in the shop this morning – her rather less communicative – and less nosy – daughter Laura served me with about as much enthusiasm as my granny had for nude bog-snorkelling but by 10 am I was sorted and ready to go.

I walked back past my cottage and along to Tony's boatyard. I went into the little office to finally pay my outstanding mooring fees and maintenance invoice. Tony was sitting at the desk with no head, surrounded by blood and brains. I ran.

Chapter 16

I untied the mooring lines and climbed aboard my boat. My head was full of fear – my body was going into shock. I couldn't remember how to start the engines. I forced myself to think and act rationally enough to get her started and pulled out of the yard into the River Bure. I kept the speed low – no more than 5 knots and moved into the centre of the water.

I was about a quarter of a mile from my cottage when I changed my mind and turned back. I had been in this situation before and made the decision to run. I had regretted it. I would not make the same mistake again – I would do what any normal member of the public would do – phone the police.

I moored the boat in Tony's yard and ran back home. Once inside I didn't hesitate – I dialled 999 and reported that I had found a headless body in the boatyard. They took my details, told me to wait at home – not to go back to the crime scene unless asked to do so by the investigating officers.

Twenty minutes later I heard sirens. The lane next to my cottage and Tony's boatyard quickly filled with emergency vehicles – mainly police, plus a couple of ambulances. Why they thought they would need two of them was beyond me.

There was a knock on my door and a tubby man in a raincoat introduced himself as Detective Chief Inspector King of Norwich CID. He asked me to come with him and we walked down to the boatyard which was buzzing with coppers and medical people.

A man in a smart suit who looked like a stray accountant, came towards us as we approached.

"Mr Garvie?" he enquired in a cultured voice.

"Yes"

"It was you who discovered the body and rang the police?"

"Yes"

"And can you verify that the deceased is one Tony Smith – owner of this marine establishment?"

"No" He looked surprised by my answer. "All I can say is that the body looked similar to Tony's but given that the head is missing I cannot verify that it is him – though I suspect that it is"

"I see"

"I don't think I got your name"

"Harvey"

"Harvey what?" his close to the chest attitude was starting to get on my wick"

"Chief Superintendent Harvey"

"Traffic control?"

He gave me a wry smirk. "Special Branch"

"Got any identification?" He begrudgingly took a card out of his inside pocket and showed it to me – it confirmed what he had said.

"OK?"

"Well, that's one little mystery we've cleared up at least" I was fed up with pussyfooting around – bollocks to the lot of them – if they wanted to suspect I had anything to do with it good luck to them proving it – my days of running scared were over. The thing about running scared is it never gets you anywhere.

I spent the next twenty minutes explaining how I had been preparing to take my boat out and had popped

85

in to say goodbye to Tony and pay him a cheque for work he had done for me. He grunted and asked me how long I had known Tony and if I knew of anyone who might be inclined to kill him. Had I seen anyone suspicious in the locality recently – that kind of thing.

After taking my contact details – address and home phone number, He said I could go and I went. I was not sure if it would look right if I buggered off in my boat right now. I thought maybe I'd wait until the circus had left town and then slip away. I had not been told I couldn't leave the area – or the country for that matter so I still had options.

I didn't doubt for one second that it was only a matter of time for the repercussions to arrive – as well as the press. It wouldn't take long for some bright spark to link me to the other occasions when I had discovered headless corpses of people I knew. I hoped I could slink off before that happened.

I waited until I saw some of the police cars and both ambulances pass my house on their way back up the track to the main road and nipped down to have a peek at what was going on. One police car and a dark Volvo – probably belonging to Harvey.

I went back home, made sure everything was as I wanted to leave it. It was. I sat, watching for the last two vehicles to leave which they did quite soon.

Then it was a case of locking up and running to *Valerie II*. I dumped my rucksack in the main lounge and climbed up to the flybridge. The engines fired into life instantly and they sounded sweet. I pulled out into the Bure once again and felt pleased that I was free and clear – at least for now. Better this way than my previous idea of going on the run. From now on whatever came my

86

way I would play it straight and take the consequences. Cloak and dagger wasn't my style.

It was dark by the time I had navigated my way back through the winding narrows that constitute the River Bure – in places my boat felt nervous – or maybe that was just me.

As I turned into the much larger River Yare at Great Yarmouth I began to relax. It was not long before I left land behind and was once again making my way into the North Sea on a Northerly bearing.

My destination was unknown and my speed slow – a calm and peaceful 20 knots in a sea which was beginning to build and swell beneath my craft. The Shipping Forecast had predicted a weak gale within three hours but I knew my boat was more than capable of dealing with that.

I had enough fuel in the tanks, plus extra jerry cans, to get a fair distance – depending on the speed – I thought it would be nice to go to Denmark and just chill there for a while. I had been there before and knew a couple of Danish sailors who lived near the coast. A good place to refuel at least and give me time to think about my next move.

The twists and turns my life was taking were unfathomable to me. Who on earth would want to kill Tony Smith? And in such a dramatic – and symbolic – manner. My first thought was Mark Hopkins – but he was dead – I had seen his smashed corpse in a warehouse in St. Malo. Then again, I had seen Johnny Walsh's corpse once upon a time and that had been a fairy story – he was still alive and a very different person to the one I had known – or thought I'd known – since childhood.

My mind reeled – it is impossible to stay calm when things are far different from what your eyes tell you – a kind of foggy, grey terror crept across my skull and infiltrated every molecule of my body and mind – in fact the fear stretched out past my physical self and attached itself to everything – inanimate objects began to hold a deep menace – their corners were sharper, their solid deadness a call from an isolated grave. Horror dripped from the very air and I had no choice but to suck it into my bloodstream.

I shook myself out of my nightmare, went below to get a shot of Captain Morgan's Spiced Rum and some ice. I drank the burning liquid – only when it hit my stomach was I aware of it. A tightening of sinews – and nerve – helped me calm myself a little and a cigarette did the rest. I would need to be made of rock and iron if I was to have any chance of getting to the bottom of the situation and finishing it forever. I cared not what would happen – only that it would happen at my hand – no more playing other people's games – I would do things my way – and if I survived, I would disappear off the map permanently.

Chapter 17

I spent the next four hours guiding my boat through increasingly heavy seas and winds – *Valerie II* pitched and rolled like a cork in a pan of boiling water but no damage was incurred if you discount some cups which fell out of a cupboard in the galley.

Once the storm had moved on, I took some readings and found that we had drifted a little towards the coast of Holland. I made the necessary adjustments and set the auto pilot in motion.

This gave me time to walk around the deck, to check the equipment and fittings on the boat. Part of the flybridge canopy had come adrift from its post and it took me half an hour or so to reattach it securely. I restacked some fuel cans and ropes which had spread themselves around the aft deck. I regreased the spring line pulleys and brushed some flotsam back into the sea from whence it had come.

I descended into the chart room – a grand name for the tiny cubbyhole which housed my geographic and weather-related equipment and manuals. I smoked and drank tea while making plans and plotting courses on charts. The information would be fed into the steering console and allow me to stay on course as the guidance system made automatic adjustments for wind strength and ocean currents – fairly accurately most of the time.

According to my calculation I should be approaching the Danish coast in about eight hours. It would be light by then and I planned to pull into a little port somewhere and spend the day buying food supplies.

I was getting low on bread, milk, ham, cigarettes and rum, which was totally unacceptable in my opinion.

I spent time thinking about the situation I was in. It was a recurring nightmare – what on earth was it all about and who was behind it? It must be someone with a personal grudge against me. Which meant somebody who knew me well enough to have personal ill-will. Most of the people I knew to be mixed up in this were dead – there were only three possibles.

First there was Johnny Walsh himself. He had told me how he had faked his own death in the exact manner that later Art Mercer – and now Tony Smith had been killed. He was also heavily involved in some high-powered game of Secret Service/Crime Syndicate which was confirmed by not only his knowledge of what had happened from the start – but also his access to the Red Boat, and the fact that he had met me in the Azores.

His story about how he had started his own personal section of M.I.6. - code-named G10 – and how it was a cover for the crime cartel sounded too crazy to be true apart from the fact that an ex-Special Branch Inspector named Glaze had been involved – also, I had met him in Whitehall at one point.

The access to information, men and weapons also supported his claims. There was no doubt that G10 existed. Whether it was ultimately run by the Secret Service – or the crime gang was yet to be discovered. It was just as likely to be both.

Johnny Walsh was definitely the most likely candidate – but why Kill Tony Smith? – and in such a manner? And why not kill me? I knew too much.

After Johnny, I began to clutch at straws – my options became implausible – mind you the whole scenario had been far-fetched from the outset – so maybe I needed to use my imagination rather than rely on facts – which had a habit of turning on their heads at short notice.

Liam Harries – the killer cop – locked up in prison for the next 30 years or more, did not seem a good candidate. Then again, Johnny had told me he was in fact not a cop killer at all, that he had protected my sister and her lads from assassination and that he was in fact a deep undercover agent for G10.

It sounded crazy but everything was crazy now. I only had Johnny's word for it that Liam Harries was anything other than the killer he was convicted of being in the courts. He had shot at me when I dived off the boat. He had also missed with two bullets. He hadn't killed his hostages when the police raided his uncle's house – he had just escaped. He would have to remain an unknown quantity. The fact that he was locked up in a high security prison made me think he wasn't going round blowing people's heads off.

My third suspect stretched the realms of credibility to breaking point. I had seen the headless body of Art Mercer with my own eyes – but I had also seen the headless body of Johnny Walsh with my own eyes.

Johnny had informed me that Mark Hopkins had killed Art – and it was certain that he would be capable of it – but it was possible that Art's body was a 'plant' just like Johnny's had been? Mark Hopkins would go along with any crazy scheme if it served his purposes.

Johnny had said that Art was involved with him in whatever it was they were involved in, so it was possible – however unlikely - that they would pull the 'headless corpse' trick more than once – it was obviously a favourite ruse of somebody. Had they given me notice that they were still around - and one step ahead of the authorities - with the killing of poor Tony Smith?

There was no way I would be able to find out the truth on my own. I could think it through until doomsday and it would be no more than speculation. I needed to find someone who might know more than me – and was likely to give me some straight answers rather than the gobbledegook and bullshit I had received from those people I had been involved with so far. Was there such a person? They would not need to be in possession of all the facts – I doubted if anyone was – but would need to know the underlying nature of this insane and bloody series of events I had been caught up in.

I no longer had any faith in Johnny Walsh. He was too deeply involved and I suspected he was behind the killing of Tony – though for the life of me I could think of no reason for it.

Art Mercer was probably dead – or if not, his whereabouts were unknown to me and would probably remain so.

Which left Liam Harries.

Chapter 18

I spent a pleasant few days in a small coastal town in Denmark; filled up on supplies; went for long walks in the countryside; chatted happily to normal people – locals and tourists – in cosy bars, and slept well. I couldn't stop concerns and questions from racing around my head but I was distracted from time to time.

It was just getting light as I piloted *Valerie II* out of the small marina and back into the North Sea. The weather was a little blustery and the boat was bobbing up and down on the growing swell.

As I moved out into the open sea, I caught a glimpse of another craft moving out behind me in the distance. It was travelling fast and veered away from me, heading Northwest, disappearing into the spray. It would have made a nice change to travel with another vessel in sight, particularly with the wind getting up but I was destined to travel the vast waterway alone – and I didn't really mind that much – alone meant safe.

Visibility worsened as I moved south. I slowed my boat to a crawl. The Shipping Forecast stated that sea areas Dogger, Forties and Viking would experience gale force 5 or 6, variable, becoming northerly 6. Sea state was moderate, becoming rough, possibly very rough later. Rain expected, visibility poor, occasionally very poor.

I would skirt those areas, staying mainly in German Bight, Humber and Thames, where the bad weather was predicted to be less and variable. My boat was more than capable under these conditions and I did not suffer from seasickness under most circumstances and certainly not in a force 5. I had been in much bigger seas and had suffered no more than a slight dizziness as my boat had pitched and rolled dramatically as the sea smashed the deck and made the fittings creak.

The weather was meant to clear by the middle of the afternoon and I should then have calm seas and good visibility all the way home.

Valerie II began to buck in the water as the wind picked up. I went below – set my course on the auto pilot and sat in the lounge, smoking and drinking a few glasses of Captain Morgan's Spiced. I dozed – the increasing rocking of the boat lulled me to sleep like a baby in a crib.

I awoke in pain and confusion – my face hitting the edge of the metal and glass coffee table. I had been thrown onto it by the extreme pitching and rolling of my boat. The sound of the storm, which had moved and strengthened from its predicted course was battering *Valerie II* hard and she wasn't enjoying the experience.

I cursed the Met Office and their forecast and hung on to a leg of the table – which was fixed to the deck – as another massive wave hit, throwing the boat around like a toy in a bathtub. The yawing motion which accompanied this wave flipped me across the room and smashed me into the portside wall of the lounge – this twisting motion increased the disorientation I was beginning to feel. I clung to the handle of a cupboard until it subsided.

There was nothing I could do but hang on and hope that I and my boat would survive the massive impacts. By my estimation this storm was at least a force 9 – maybe a full-on cyclone. We were spinning like we were going down the plug hole – I didn't know how wide a cyclonic wind system was or how long it would last – my experience of such things was nil. I presumed that,

94

just like a tornado over a land mass, a cyclone would have a calm central area called an eye – though this was pure speculation on my part. Even though I had spent a few years pottering about in boats, I had never experienced truly bad weather. It was not a situation I was enjoying. The way the boat was rolling from side to side, I thought it likely she would capsize sooner rather than later.

Another huge wave crashed over the deck, causing the craft to wallow deeply – water began to pour into the lounge and then washed back out as the boat tipped the other way.

I scrambled and crawled my way through the door which led to the communications cubby hole and slammed it behind me. I braced against the wall as the boat twisted and pitched so violently that I was thrown in the air and landed against the radio console, cracking my head on a corner of the metal casing. I felt blood dripping down the left side of my face and curled up in a ball on the floor.

For the next twenty minutes – which seemed like twenty hours – I was tossed and twisted, bashed and smashed like a ping pong ball in a tumble drier – my head taking three more violent hits – one of which made my brain go funny as my consciousness began to fade.

I came back to what passed for reality sometime later. It must have been quite a while because the boat was now considerably calmer – it was still rocking and rolling but the twisting, yawing motion was gone.

I hoped this was not just an 'eye' which would soon pass, leading to another episode of life-threatening, hurricane-force winds. I righted the upturned stool and placed it in front of the radio controls. Grabbing the handset, I clicked the side button and sent out a call on an open channel to see if anyone else in the vicinity knew if the storm was over or just having a little rest before getting back on the job with full fury. I heard static – nothing more. After two more attempt I assumed the radio was broken or that there was nobody within range.

I stood up and opened the door – water washed in and went over my feet.

"Bollocks!" I exclaimed.

The lounge was underwater to a depth of about six inches. I ran up to the main deck and saw that my boat was very deep in the water. Too deep.

I descended the steps which led to the engine room in the lower deck – water had got in and was up to my waist. I waded over to the bilge pump control and opened the bilges to full. The pump motors sounded like they were about to give up the ghost but began pumping the water out slowly. I had a horrible feeling they would not last much longer and thought it unlikely my boat would be going anywhere fast – unless it was the bottom of the sea.

The engines were spluttering as the water did more damage with every passing moment. How long they would function at all was anybody's guess.

I looked at the global positioning read-out – it was flashing on and off but while it was on it was telling me we were about 5 miles off the German coast. I re-set the auto pilot to head for the East Frisian islands and hoped it was still working correctly. I felt *Valerie II* change course immediately – which indicated that the auto pilot was indeed working.

I went up top and waded through knee-high water as I crossed to the prow. There was not as much damage to be seen as I had expected but that was because most of the fixtures and fittings which had been destroyed by the storm had been washed overboard. The flybridge was smashed to buggery and the upper deck seating was gone. Pulleys were twisted and one of the telecommunication aerials was bent dramatically. There was seaweed strewn on the main deck and the glass doors at the top of the steps leading to the main lounge were broken. There was a half-dead octopus squeezed behind the upper fuel storage cradle – no doubt washed aboard at the height of the storm – I picked it up and threw it back into its preferred habitat.

"Good Luck mate" I called, as its angry body flew through the air before plopping back into the water.

We were still far too low in the water and the engines had started struggling – not yet cutting out but seriously thinking about it. The engine room would have to be completely overhauled when – and if – I ever got *Valerie II* back into dock.

I perched on the starboard gunwale and looked out to sea as we slowly fought our way through still high seas towards the North German coast.

An hour later I made out an island – the visibility had improved as I approached land and the water was a lot calmer too. My boat was still grinding along – no more than 10 knots now – we were getting within hoping distance. I myself should make land at any rate – even if the boat's engines packed up – and who could blame them – I could drop my small rubber dinghy in the water and paddle the rest of the way to the harbour I saw growing in size as we got nearer. My guess was that the island was Norderney – approximately 8 miles long and two miles wide – half of which is a national park of some sort.

I switched off the auto pilot, took over the steering from the battered flybridge and headed towards a small marina. I slipped into a mooring position near the harbour entrance.

I then spent over an hour getting permissions and signing documents which the rather unimpressed harbour master insisted I complete before taking a payment from me to cover my mooring for one week.

Seeing the state of my boat – and my bleeding head - he was concerned that I would find it difficult to get her seaworthy in such a short time and wanted to avoid getting lumbered with a deserted wreck. I finally convinced him that I would be contacting 'my team' and they would soon have her 'shipshape and Bristol fashion' again – a phrase which brought a look of bafflement to his frustrated visage.

I took the regular local ferry, which runs to and from Norddeich Pier and was soon in the small mainland town of Norden.

From there I took a coach to Hamburg – and then a regular flight to Gatwick brought me back to England. It was time to face the music…

Chapter 19

My first port of call after arriving back in Norfolk, was home. It didn't feel like home though – I had a strong feeling of paranoia resting in my brain – its grey twitching tendrils creeping down my shoulders and neck.

I carefully unlocked my front door – half expecting a bomb to explode or a shotgun to blast my head off. Nothing happened. I carefully searched each room and checked outdoors and my garden shed. No killers detected.

I went back inside and poured a stiff drink - Morgan's to the rescue – not for the first time. My mind was busy – I interrupted its cloudy concerns and forced myself to come up with a plan of action – action is the only thing which blows fear away, in my opinion – though the effect is only temporary and partial.

I had to act quickly. Whoever was behind it all – and I had less and less of a clue as to what 'it all' was any more – would be several steps ahead of me if previous events were anything to go by. I may have a chance if I did something extremely unexpected – though I could think of nothing to fit that category at present.

I decided to contact Harries – if I could get a pass to visit him in prison. He was deeply involved in the situation and might be aware of what was going on behind the scenes at a more fundamental level than I was.

Johnny Walsh had told me that Harries was now an undercover agent – I was not sure exactly who he was an agent for – or even if this was true – but I had very limited options, so I was willing to try to find out what he had to say.

According to Walsh, Harries had been transferred to the High Security Unit of HMP Bellmarsh which was situated at Thamesmead in south-east London. This was reputedly the most secure prison in the whole of the UK.

I picked up the phone and asked the operator for the number of the prison. She gave me the number of the general switchboard which I rang. I was transferred to the Visitors' Department.

I was asked numerous questions about who I was and my reasons for the visit request. I told them I was an acquaintance of the prisoner's and had important news for him which it would not be appropriate to pass on over the phone or by letter.

They told me to wait while they spoke to the prisoner to see if he would accept my visit. I hung up and waited nervously for about twenty minutes before they rang back and gave me a Visitor's Pass Number – this was encouraging because from what I could gather you normally had to wait until the pass was sent to you by post – which could take three or four days – sometimes more. This indicated that Harries was keen to speak to me. Maybe I was clutching at straws. At least I still had a couple of straws to clutch at.

I was to see the prisoner at 10am the following morning and to this end I left the house and drove to Norwich station. From there I got a London train to Liverpool Street, before booking into a hotel near Woolwich, next to the Ferry terminal. It wasn't five star.

By nine the next morning I was sitting in a greasy spoon drinking orange builder's tea and stuffing bacon rolls down my neck. The place was full of smoke, so I added some of my own. From here it was a five-minute walk to Bellmarsh and I intended to arrive there early.

100

It took nearly an hour to get to where I needed to be – what with queues, security checks, searches, people asking for identification and seemingly pointless questions – and long walks down iron corridors through a maze of passages, metal doors, gates, keys, warders, noise, heat and nasty human smells.

Finally, I was shown into a small room containing a small metal table – fixed to the floor with bolts – two metal chairs likewise affixed - and no windows. It was more of a cell than a room and it was hot.

Sitting on one of the chairs and staring straight at me was Liam Harries. Last time I had seen him was when he held me at gunpoint and used me as a hostage in a seaborne police shootout scenario. Those were the days!

Liam had changed significantly during his five years in this prison full of hard cases. He looked more than five years older – his hair was darker and longer and his face was filled with tension. No more the jolly carefree cop killer and kidnapper I used to know in the good old days. Here was a man who had made some very bad decisions and looked like he knew it.

I sat in the only available chair, facing Harries. We didn't shake hands.

"Thanks for agreeing to see me". He shrugged.

"I wasn't doing anything special today – so why not?" I forced a smile. I lit up a cigarette. Offered him one. He declined.

"If you don't mind, I would like to ask you some questions"

"If I do mind, I won't answer them"

"Fair enough. Before we start – are we being listened to in here?"

"No, it's private. We jailbirds do have some rights left" He grinned cynically.

"Glad to hear it. Firstly, I'd like to know why you shot those coppers and abducted my family?"

"Wouldn't you rather start at the beginning – as the old cliché goes?"

"Nope – I want to know why you shot those coppers and abducted my family". I wanted to know if what Johnny Walsh had told me about the incident was true or not.

"I really think you would need some background information before I answer your question". I shook my head.

"I got reasons for asking this first – and I have a lot more background information than you might think. I'm hoping you can help me arrange that information into some sort of order, fill in a few blank areas".

"Ok then, we'll play it your way for now"

"I appreciate it".

"I was undercover – deep undercover"

"In what way?"

"The British Secret Service has many operations ongoing at all times – some of which are not made known to agents involved in other operations running simultaneously. So, what can happen is one 'cell' can come up against another 'cell' without either side knowing that the other is on the same side".

"Sounds likely" I quipped.

"None of my colleagues in the Flying Squad knew I was anything other than Detective Sergeant Harries but I was in fact working for a Top-Secret group known as G10". I laughed humourlessly.

"Yeah, I've met them – a nice bunch of psychopaths"

He laughed in agreement – it was the first time I had seen him break the tension which surrounded him. "That's an accurate description" He said. I stubbed out my cigarette.

"Why were you undercover in a police squad? – seems odd – unless you suspected somebody was bent"

"Access to information – we needed to know what the Sweeney knew as soon as they knew it – they were in charge of the investigation into certain activities with which G10 were involved – by having someone inside the police operation we could react quickly to any event or info which might help or harm our mission". I almost laughed out loud at the word 'mission' – it sounded to me like Liam was living a cinema spy movie fantasy – but I guess nobody's perfect.

"So, you were just a fly on the wall so to speak?"

"Exactly"

"So, what turned you from passive observer to active cop shooter and kidnapper?" It sounded brutal but I wanted my question answered and I was fed up with the niceties of the conversation. He grimaced at my words and a look of anger flashed across his once-boyish face.

"You don't know what you're talking about Garvie!" he raised his voice and pushed on the table like he was going to get up and leave.

"That's why I'm here Harries – to find out why you acted in the way you did – no offence mate but I've got a train to catch in six hours!" Luckily for me he laughed at that and relaxed into his chair again.

"It may surprise you to know but I was actually the good guy – don't believe what you read in the papers – ever!"

"I never do"

"I found out that certain persons were going to kill your sister and her two kids – so I went down there to keep an eye open. They made their move – I stopped them and took the hostages to a place of safety"

"Your uncle Leo's house – called 'Fleetwood'. I remember you jumping out of a window and forcing me at gunpoint to drive you to the seaside".

"Yes, that was fun wasn't it" he grinned "I had to maintain my cover – G10 wanted me as deep as I could get. I managed to save your relatives from the hit man, whilst simultaneously making myself look like a hardened criminal – I planned to get to France where G10 were aware of a major drug ring"

"St. Malo" I replied. He looked surprised.

"You know about St. Malo?" I nodded.

"I know a lot of things – you'd be surprised"

"Well as you know – I never made it to France – my hostage messed up my escape by diving into the sea!"

"Sorry about that!" We both laughed. I lit up another cigarette – this time he had one too.

"I couldn't infiltrate the gang from prison but I knew they would be aware of my behaviour and they would also have discovered that I was Leo Thomas' nephew. Leo was involved in the drug smuggling but didn't like the violence – he wanted out when it got nasty – but it's not easy to resign from the syndicate. He had saved your sorry arse when Hopkins rammed your boat. Hopkins was not amused and promised he'd catch up with Leo some time".

104

"Which I can confirm that he has – permanently" Harries looked downcast. Not surprised or shocked.

"I knew he was dead – the governor of this five-star hotel informed me personally – though I didn't get all the details. I had assumed it was Hopkins or one of his associates who had killed Leo"

"It was Hopkins *and* some of his associates – including Ex-Detective Inspector Glaze of Special Branch – now G10!" Harries looked surprised now. And shocked.

"You're sure about this?" he asked.

"I was there myself when it happened. It was a G10 operation. I was in G10 myself at the time – who knows, maybe I still am"

"Why would G10 kill him?"

"It's a long and very convoluted story mate – I was hoping you could help me to un-convolute it a bit"

"I have not heard from G10 for a while – I seem to be out of the loop stuck in here"

"We're all out of the loop now mate" I said, cryptically.

"What do you mean?"

"What I mean is that all the members of G10 that I ever met or was made aware of are now dead" He went pale.

"Are you sure?"

"As sure as I can be of anything anymore"

"All of them?"

"Everyone I knew to be G10 – but obviously there may be more who I do not know"

"Is Glaze dead?" he enquired – his voice shaking now.

"Definitely – he was blown to bits with Mark Hopkins and some others in a massive gunfight in St. Malo. I was outside in a van when the explosion happened – I went in and saw what was left of the bodies"

"Glaze is definitely dead though?"

"Yes – I already told you" I snapped at him "Why do you keep going on about Glaze for God's sake?"

"Because he was one of only two people who knew I was a member of G10 – if he has been killed and not told anyone else that I am an undercover agent – and the second man cannot be found, then I'm stuck here for the rest of my life!"

"I take your point." I quipped. He rolled his eyes.

"I may be in more trouble than I thought – and that was plenty," said Harries.

"I know the feeling".

I decided it was time to change the subject. "What do you know about the shooting of Johnny Walsh?" He laughed out loud and shook his head from side to side.

"Johnny Walsh faked his own death. Johnny Walsh is the head of G10"

"Or the head of the drug syndicate" I countered.

"Or both!" we both said in unison".

Chapter 20

I spent over two hours in that little room, talking to Liam Harries. He was a broken, scared and forgotten man. G10 – whoever and whatever they were – had made use of him and when he needed them most, they abandoned him.

They had done the same to me – getting me involved in all kinds of deadly escapades and then keeping me out of the loop, ploughing through with their bloody games with no thought for their own operatives – or anyone who got in their way.

Just like Liam Harries I was no longer in contact with anyone from G10 – I didn't even know if they still existed – and I certainly didn't see them coming to my rescue should I need it.

Harries was in far deeper trouble than I was – he was a convicted police killer and there was only one person still alive who knew his true identity as an undercover operative for the British Secret Service – if indeed G10 were actually what it claimed to be rather than a false cover for the drug smuggling organisation.

The only other person I knew to be involved and still alive was Johnny Walsh. He had known all about the Red Boat and the shoot-out in St. Malo. I suspected he was the 'second man' who knew about Liam Harries' true identity. That he was involved in the G10 project was indisputable. That he was also involved in the drug cartel was likewise beyond question. He seemed to have the knack of weaving elaborate narratives which got people involved in extreme actions. Was he ultimately a good guy or a villain? There was, as things currently stood, no way of knowing. He was out of the picture – his whereabouts a mystery. No doubt he was plotting his next event – he never let the grass grow under his feet. I had a horrible feeling he would ensure I was involved in it somehow – he had dragged me into his web continually since that first day, when I discovered his headless corpse in his house – the whole thing a set-up from the beginning. I had made things worse for myself no doubt but Johnny had kept me alive as best he could – at least that was the story he told me when I met him in the Azores.

I had believed his story – right up until I found Tony Smith's headless corpse in the boatyard – that piece of theatre had all the hallmarks of a Walsh set-up. I now didn't trust my old friend at all, but for the life of me I could think of not a single reason why Johnny would act like this towards me – it seemed odd to say the least. We had always been friends and never had so much as a serious argument in all the time we had known each other. There had to be more to it. It didn't add up.

My thinking was taking shape – though it was a very odd shape indeed. I placed Johnny Walsh firmly in the 'probably bad' category and Liam Harries in the 'probably good'. This in itself was weird because my oldest friend was looking like an enemy – and a very dangerous one at that – whereas the man who had kidnapped my sister and her kids, who had abducted me at gunpoint and shot at me, was now potentially an ally.

My main enemy of the past few years – Mark Hopkins was dead – as were most of the people I had become involved with – entangled might be a more accurate description – since my troubles began.

It looked like I was in the clear now, regarding the police - I hoped so anyway. It was possible that they may want to question me further regarding the recent murder of Tony Smith – I might even have to be a witness in court – but I didn't feel like I was on the wanted list anymore.

The crime cartel – the people running the international drug smuggling operation were in disarray – at least I suspected as much considering the damage done to them by the G10 mission I had been part of recently.

If, as I suspected, Johnny Walsh wanted to get out of the racket, whilst simultaneously eliminating any ambitious rivals who might want to make trouble for him – then he had done a good job. Most people thought he was dead – any who may have known or believed any different were splattered over half the European continent. If it hadn't been for the way that Tony Smith had been killed, I would have felt that Johnny was still on my side. I suppose someone else could have been behind it but it seemed that Walsh had been at least one step ahead all along and I could think of nobody – except Hopkins – who was blown to bits – who would have had the twisted sense of humour to carry out this unnecessary and symbolic killing of an innocent man.

There was one more thing I wanted to do before I set sail forever to some far-off land of sun, sand and silence. I had to make sure – if I could – that Art Mercer was actually dead. His killing had so many similarities to the fake murder of Johnny Walsh that a part of me wondered if Mercer was actually still alive – maybe in league with Walsh all along – maybe his enemy.

I had read about the killing in the papers at the time it happened but they mainly described *me* as the fugitive suspect hunted by the entire British police force – that was old news – I was no longer suspected – it was

109

generally believed that Mark Hopkins had done it – he was there at the time I discovered the body and had a shotgun with him. To be honest I no longer gave a rat's arse who had killed him – I just wanted to make sure it wasn't another elaborate hoax. If I could make sure Art *was* dead it would be one less variable I would have to juggle.

Things seemed to be getting, if not clearer, at least less complex – mainly because so many of the people involved were no longer living. Walsh, Mercer, Harries – I had it narrowed down to three, based on the assumption that I wasn't too far out of the loop and off the mark - that there wasn't a whole higher level of operation to this thing than I could have suspected. Which had been pretty much par for the course up until now.

I would have to follow where my information took me. I would gain nothing by speculation about G10 or by wondering how many other layers there were to the drug cartel's management. At least not now. I needed action, movement.

Chapter 21

I drove my old Land Rover 200 miles south-west and arrived in Southampton around noon. Art Mercer's place was boarded up. It looked as if it had been like that for five years. It probably had.

I wandered around the perimeter of the premises and saw nothing of significance – it was just an old, closed-down garage with pallets, engine parts and an old rusting Ford Cortina in the forecourt. I had no way of knowing what was inside – I didn't want to think about the last time I was in there. Art Mercer was gone – probably dead – if not, he was far away from this building – which was the only link to him I had.

I drove all the way back to Norfolk and spent a sleepless night, my mind re-playing events I would rather forget. It was too hot and there was no breeze. I was glad when it got light, so I could tell myself it was morning and get up – it was 4am.

I took a cold shower – I had forgotten to put the boiler on. I ate a ham sandwich I had bought at a filling station on the way home yesterday – it was horrible. I drank two cups of coffee, smoked three cigarettes, mooched around the house – making sure everything was shipshape. I made sure I had my passport, credit cards, cash and other essentials in my ruck sack.

At 6.20am I climbed into my Land Rover and drove away again – who knew when I would be back to my little cottage. I sure as hell didn't.

I hoped that one day I would be able to live in peace here but had a persistent feeling that for some reason I would not be permitted to do so.

111

As things stood, there was nothing I could do about it. The puppet master – who I believed to be Johnny Walsh – had faded into the background – I had no way of contacting him. Harries was in no position to do anything and Mercer even less so.

My only sensible option was to retrieve my boat from Germany and go sailing. I wanted to get far away from land – and the humans who infested it - and stay there.

I got a train from Norwich to London. Another to Gatwick and a scheduled flight to Hamburg. It was dark by the time I arrived in a taxi in the town of Norden. I booked into a small, smart hotel and slept peacefully.

After a much-needed German-style buffet breakfast which included crisp rolls, hams, cheeses and peach nectar, I walked onto the small terrace which looked out on the little bustling town. The sense of order, cleanliness and efficiency which permeates small German towns was a delight to see and I almost booked to stay for a few more days.

In the end I decided I could always come back at a later stage if I wanted. I needed to get my boat sorted out before the man who ran the marina blew a fuse. He had not been impressed with the semi-wreck I had left in his tidy harbour; the fact that my 'team' would not have materialised – mainly because they were made up and didn't exist – would have made him even less impressed. I checked out of the hotel and caught a local bus to the Norddeich Pier Ferry.

Just before noon I arrived at the marina. My boat was gone. The man told me that 'my team' had fixed her up and paid the bill before sailing off into the sunset – this was two days ago. I didn't bother getting angry or

112

explaining that my boat had been stolen – I knew by now that I would get no help from the authorities – I was on my own.

I went back to Norden and re-booked into the hotel. I would stay for two nights, try to clear my head and come up with yet another vague plan based on incomplete facts and confused fears - it was futile but I didn't see what else I could do.

That evening I had a nice meal in the hotel before visiting a couple of quiet bars. The normality was good for me. I needed it.

I went back to the hotel around 10pm and had a double brandy in the bar. An attractive blonde looked at me in a way I would have liked under normal circumstances – but now I just saw it as suspicious. I had become paranoid – or had I? Is it paranoia if there really are people out to get you? Probably not. I scuttled off to my room, locked the door, checked the window was shut and fell into a troubled sleep.

The next day was Sunday. Most of the shops were closed. German towns, although attractive, could be very dull if they felt like it – which they often did. There is a thin line between peace and quiet and outright boredom. I spent the day switching from one side of that line to the other and back again.

In the evening I avoided the hotel bar. I had some unexciting food in an unexciting little restaurant and walked around the town, enjoying the cool evening breeze. I was in bed by 10pm and slept a little better than the previous night – although I was wide awake by 6am.

After a shower and a smoke, I went down to the dining room and enjoyed my breakfast in a room with only one other person in it. I was early. The waiter seemed a little miffed that people were here before he was ready for them – they were disrupting his methodical routine.

After breakfast I spent an hour strolling around the town, watching it come to life. Then I went back to my room, grabbed my bag and checked out.

By 9am I was standing at the railway station, waiting for the Hamburg Express which was on time.

I sat in a seat at the far end of an almost empty carriage and watched 184 km of scenery pass by.

When we got to Hamburg Hauptbanhof in just under three and a half hours. The place was filled with noise and people being busy. I drank a cup of strong coffee in a snack bar in the station before filing out into the warm, hectic streets of the city.

I wandered around, acting the part of a tourist, looking at the sights, walking around modern, efficient shopping centres, popping into quaint little cafés. By 3pm I was bored stiff and my head was back into its churning motion – going over things which were only half-remembered, half-understood and unfathomable.

I was out of the game. My head just wouldn't let go. Someone was playing with me. I suspected Johnny Walsh – my mind was sick of Johnny Walsh – sick of dead people, sick of the police, sick of courts, sick of crime bosses and guns and fake coppers and fake criminals and secret organisations which may or may not even exist. It was too much. I'd had it. I refused to play their game any longer – but I could not think of any way to move on from it. Even if I went off to the Sahara Desert, my thoughts would still be there – my confusion would remain, my growing sense of anger at being made a fool of so many times by so many people was beginning to build a reckless urge to force an ending even if it was the end of me.

My boat was gone. I hoped it was Johnny Walsh who had taken it – he certainly seemed to have the resources and inside information required to get things done. I wanted it to be one of Johnny's little jokes. Because if it wasn't Johnny, it was someone else – and that would be even more worrying.

It might mean that the crime guys were coming after me – or G10 were still in operation – or some other fucking nest of psychopaths was playing games at my expense. It almost drove me mad. I felt hunted, lost, depressed - full of rage and despair.

I had to get out of Hamburg – it was too big, too noisy – my mind needed peace, isolation, open spaces.

I made my way to the airport and booked myself on a flight to Norway. It was shit or bust again. Again.

Chapter 22

The Red Boat was moored, innocent and quiet, where I had last seen her. The town of Henningsvær was still cool and peaceful. There were fewer tourists now as the temperature and light levels were starting to drop as the year moved from high summer towards the coolness of autumn.

I walked along the jetty and bounded straight onto the lower deck of the boat. I tried the door to the main cabin – it was locked. I forced it open and went inside. The room was empty. I bundled my way down to the lower deck, the engine room, galley and chart room. The boat was unoccupied. The layer of dust on the coffee table in the lounge suggested it had been unoccupied for some time.

I went into the wheelhouse and threw my rucksack onto one of the hard seats. They keys were there. I said, "Here Goes nothing" and started the engines. They roared into life. I went back onto the jetty and unhitched the spring lines.

It took me two minutes to re-acquaint myself with the controls. Then I was moving out of the little harbour – out into open water. The wind was low, the craft bobbed only a little as I approached the three-mile limit and left Norwegian waters for international ones.

I decided I would stay on this boat for as long as possible – if someone came to stop me, I would resist. If someone got in my way, I would show no mercy. I would go far away. I had no plans to make any plans. They owed me a boat. I now had one.

The North Sea was a bit choppy as I set the boat to autopilot – the sophisticated computerised system would deal easily with these seas and could adjust automatically for drift and changes in wind direction – given a location to reach, it would reach it. I had not entered a location – just set the controls to keep us moving in a westerly direction at a steady 10 knots – I was in no hurry – there was nowhere I had to be.

For three hours, the seas were calm, the sun shone, the boat moved through the water like a sleek red shark. I lazed on deck, had a couple of long drinks, ate some ham sandwiches and snoozed. It was idyllic.

As the afternoon drew to a close and evening shadows began to appear, I checked my position, set a course for just north of Lerwick and went below to get an early night. I didn't bother listening to the Shipping Forecast. I figured this high tech, super-boat should be able to cope with anything the weather gods decided to throw at her.

In the morning everything looked the same – it was light, the sun shone, the sea was calm. I had been travelling slowly. My position was now just a few miles North-West of Lerwick. There were seagulls aplenty – drawn towards the trawlers and other marine craft which sailed these waters. I thought I saw some dolphins in the distance but it may have been wishful thinking. The air temperature was low, so I put a thin jacket on to keep in some warmth.

I enjoyed a leisurely breakfast, consisting of bacon and eggs which I found in the very well-stocked provisions cupboards on the boat. There was really no need for me to go anywhere near land for several months. I couldn't think of a reason why I should.

117

I spent the day investigating the boat. There were lockers down below which contained a massive amount of weaponry, explosives, protective clothing, things which I did not recognise but which looked nasty.

There was a small dinghy with a very powerful outboard motor, some things which were probably missiles – though I couldn't see how they could be fired - medical supplies enough to satisfy a small hospital and a big library of maps and charts.

The boat was certainly designed for some special purpose – I had a hard time believing that Johnny Walsh had been behind the design of this craft. It had military government written all over it.

I also discovered a door right at the lowest level, past the engine room, positioned near the prow of the boat. A big yellow sign with an unpleasant spiky symbol and the words 'Danger' and 'Warning' liberally applied to its surface was affixed thereto. There were a couple of big white chemical protection suits hanging in a small alcove outside the door.

I tried the handle. It turned but the door wouldn't open. A red light in a small wall-mounted panel began to flash. I let go of the handle. After 30 seconds the red light stopped flashing. I moved back up top, spent some time snooping around in the wheelhouse.

Along with a lot of very modern control and safety equipment, military grade comms systems and radar, there was a console which I didn't recognise. After half an hour coming up with all kinds of ideas regarding its purpose, I decided it was something to do with the Red Boat's purported cloaking ability – whereby the craft could be made undetectable to radar, satellite or any other tracking system.

I pressed a few buttons, managed to get some green lights lit up. Whether this meant the boat could no longer be tracked – or that it could now be tracked - I didn't know. I pressed the buttons again and the lights went out. I would leave things as they were unless I thought of a good reason to change them. I had not been contacted on the radio and no helicopter gunships had appeared in the sky above – a good result by recent standards.

Later that afternoon, I passed South of the Faroe Islands and set a course South-West, heading out into the North Atlantic. The seas became rougher for a time but the boat bobbed and twisted as happy as a duck in a millpond.

I spent part of that evening looking up at the stars - much brighter and more numerous out here, far away from all the artificial lights of the human world. A large shoal of fish danced past the boat, glittering and flashing like diamonds, beneath the surface of the water.

I drank several glasses of Captain Morgan Spiced. I didn't smoke – with the pressure off I didn't feel I needed to.

I went below, fixed myself a decent meal from ingredients if found in the overstocked galley. Spaghetti Bolognaise. There was even Parmesan to sprinkle on top. I opened a bottle of Argentinian Malbec, let it breathe as I cooked, took my meal up to the aft deck and sat there like a multi-millionaire playboy aboard one of his yachts. I polished off the rest of the wine and began to dose in my chair, under the stars.

The next week was idyllic. I sailed amid mainly gentle waters, saw no other boats and had zero contact with any other human beings. I never once listened to the meteorological reports or played music on the radio. I was totally alone, miles out at sea, enjoying the absolute peace and quiet that only comes far from other life. Though of course there was life – beneath me. The ocean was teeming with it. I saw a pod of some sort of whale but they were too far off to get a clear view. There were also sea birds – including an albatross or two, a species I had never seen before, despite the time I had spent at sea.

I cooked myself a meal each evening – the fresh vegetables soon had to be replaced with frozen but there were enough rations to feed an army for a month of Sundays. I ate and drank to excess and enjoyed it immensely.

I kept the boat slow, setting a straight course to nowhere each night before I slept like a baby for a good eight hours. My thoughts became less chaotic, my mind was mending itself. I spent less time going over old ground.

I stopped shaving, started to grow a beard which I planned to keep doing until I looked like a proper salty seadog. I had no interest in what tomorrow would bring – I was happy living each day as it came.

Sometimes I sat up all night in the wheelhouse, steering the boat nowhere special, watching the light creep away and many hours later, creep back again. I slept when I felt like it. Day and night meant nothing to me. Neither did location. The only reason I ever checked my position was to ensure I had not inadvertently drifted anywhere near land. I did see ships – mainly tankers and massive container ships in the distance, ploughing heavily through the water on their endless journeys from port to port, but no small craft.

120

I was hundreds of miles from anywhere – in the middle of the North Atlantic. Here I found peace. Here I found freedom. Here I found happiness. I was surprised when they found me.

Chapter 23

The radio crackled into life, a tinny voice said "Ahoy". I seriously considered ripping the radio out and throwing it in the sea but they would not let that stop them, I knew. My luxury holiday was over. I knew that too.

"What do you want Johnny?" I said, not too friendly.

"Sorry to spoil your vacation Mike but we've got work to do"

"What have you done with my boat?"

"*Valerie II* is safely moored in Dover – all ship shape and Bristol fashion as the saying goes – no need to thank me"

"I wasn't going to"

"I suppose I can't really blame you for that – I've put you through a lot of grief recently – much of which was beyond my control though"

"Was the killing of poor Tony Smith beyond your control Johnny? Or was that a little recreational murder just to keep your hand in?"

"I didn't kill Tony Smith"

"Oh sure!"

"Seriously – I had nothing to do with that – I only heard about it after you'd gone off in your boat"

"You'll have to excuse me if I don't believe you"

"I understand. There's no way I can prove it and I wouldn't expect you to take my word for it after all the things that have happened". I had nothing to say to this so I said nothing. There was a silence which lasted no longer than ten seconds but which seemed longer. Then the Red Boat's engines stopped and there was more silence. I thought of something to say.

"I suppose that's your doing Walsh – some sort of radio control?"

"Yes… sorry to be so dramatic but like I said when I first called – we've got work to do".

"You may have work to do but I'm on holiday, so just leave me out of it. I don't want to be involved in any more of your twisted plans. I cannot believe what a megalomaniac you've become – or that you seem to have access to organisations and equipment which I've never even heard of. How the hell did things get so crazy? I realise I never knew you at all – unless you are in fact some sort of clone or robot version of the boy I went to school with?" I heard him chuckle out loud at this.

"Mike – it's not anything as mad as that – I just got involved with the Intelligence Community after I left school – obviously I couldn't tell you about it – Official Secrets Act and all that guff"

"That might explain a bit of spying, information gathering – normal undercover stuff – but it certainly doesn't begin to explain how you seem to be running both a government operation that is so secret not even the Secret Service knows about it *and* an international drug syndicate – both of which organisations seem to relish the chance to murder anyone they can get their hands on."

"It can all be explained to your satisfaction I assure you Mike – we need to meet up and I will put you fully in the picture"

"I normally just end up in the frame when I have any dealings with you Johnny". I heard him laugh again. I was glad he was finding it all so amusing.

"I cannot tell you any more now – I am going to set you a course for St. Malo. I will be waiting when you arrive"

"I can see I have no choice in the matter"

"You could always dive over the side and swim for it – I know the technique has worked well for you in the past"

"Go fuck yourself Walsh". The radio went dead. He had switched off at his end. No doubt he took my foul language as an agreement to meet him in France. We both knew my only way out of this scenario was to do as he commanded – or drown myself and get it over with once and for all. I didn't want to die yet – not until I'd made Johnny Walsh regret ever involving me in his insane schemes. All I needed was one little chance and I would finish him for good.

The boat engines started up again and the craft turned onto a North-East heading, the speed increased to over 30 knots. I went down below to retrieve my bottle of Captain Morgan Spiced Rum.

I no longer had control of the boat. It was being directed by Walsh from some super-villain lair - the location of which was possibly in or near to St. Malo – though he could travel a fair distance in the time it would take me to reach the French port. By private plane he could reach St Malo from anywhere on the globe in time to meet me. So much for speculation. He had appeared pretty quickly in the Azores when I had last met him. I would just have to wait and see what he chose to tell me. I wouldn't go along with any more of his plans unless he gave me the full story. Johnny Walsh had played games with me long enough. Either he talks or I walks.

Chapter 24

I saw Johnny Walsh standing on the jetty as the Red Boat – still controlled by some automatic guidance system – pulled up alongside and parked itself with incredible precision. It was certainly a very clever piece of kit.

Johnny hopped aboard and held out his hand for me to shake. I ignored the gesture. He shrugged and went onto the aft deck where he sat in one of the chairs and gestured for me to do likewise. I ignored the offer. I lounged against one of the gunwales and lit a cigarette. I was still a little drunk from all the rum I had necked on the journey here. I was feeling hot, angry and belligerent.

Walsh stood up again and came over to where I was. I awarded myself a point.

"Mike, I will explain everything and you can walk away if you are not completely satisfied with what I say."

"Big talk!" I sniped.

"Let's have a drink and we can get things sorted straight away" His business-like, confident manner got right under my skin – it was all just in a day's work for him. I fixed him with an angry stare.

"You really are a total prick Walsh"

"And you're just a plaything in the hands of fate – I guess nobody is perfect"

"That's the first true thing you've said – possibly ever!" I grumbled. I was feeling like a mug. I had indeed been a mere bagatelle – a fool – being moved around like a pawn on a chess board. However much I hated Johnny Walsh now, I had to admit that he had been running rings around me for years.

I have been operating on a" –

- "Need to know basis?" I finished the sentence for him. He couldn't keep a smile from creeping over his face.

"I guess you must be sick of hearing that phrase, eh?"

"Just a little"

"Well now the time has come when you need to know everything from the very beginning – nothing held back"

"I'll believe that on the day after Hell freezes over pal".

"No Mike. You will believe it at precisely the moment I finish showing you the truth. It will not be open to question"

"You wanna bet on that Walsh?"

"Yes, I do Garvie".

I walked over to the seating area and sat in the very chair that Johnny had recently vacated.

"Take a seat". I gestured to the chair next to mine. Johnny laughed out loud and did as I requested. I awarded myself another point.

I lit up another cigarette and poured myself three fingers of rum. I didn't offer any to Johnny. He could get it himself if he wanted it.

Johnny sat back in his chair. He looked calm. There was an almost military aspect to his bearing which I had never noticed before. He had obviously become very different to the man he was when I knew him. I wondered for how many years he had been living a double life – I had known him as an overalled car geek – eternally fixing that classic Ford Anglia which never seemed to be on the road for very long. Had he set up that scene each time I arranged to visit him? It was mind-boggling. If he was some sort of top-secret undercover spy – why keep in touch with me at all – why keep the house in the New Forest in Hampshire? – was it just nostalgia for the home he had grown up in? Maybe if I stopped speculating and just listened to what Johnny had to say, I would find out.

"Get on with it then, I've got things to do" I looked at my watch as I said this. I didn't want to make it easy for him. He had to pay something for all the misery he had caused me.

"When I left school, I was approached by a man in a café who offered me a job in the intelligence community"

"Oh, do fuck off!" I yelled. This sounded like the kind of story a kid would make up – and he expected me to believe that after all I had been through.

"I know it sounds mad but that did actually happen. Alright it wasn't out of the blue like I made it sound. I had been enquiring about jobs related to intelligence – the police, army and even MI5. I had a great desire to be a spy – it always appealed to me – you must remember how I used to read spy novels and watch all the espionage films on TV?"

I did actually remember that Johnny had loved anything to do with espionage when we were kids.

"Go on" I said.

"In those days, some of the recruitment people for the Secret Service used to watch people who had shown an interest and approach them if they felt that the person had some potential to be of use in an undercover situation. It was important that I retain my normal appearance and that as far as the general public – friends, neighbours, family, were concerned I was still ordinary, simple Johnny the guy who fixed cars. That was my cover."

"So, what did this guy in the café say to you?" I refilled my glass.

"After a few meetings, including a visit to the headquarters of MI5 which blew me away and dispelled any small concerns I might have had, I was taken on to their Induction Course. The preliminary training is used to weed out any prospective agents who showed bad judgement or other weakness which could be a major vulnerability when working undercover"

"So obviously you passed with flying colours?"

"Well, I passed – let's just say that. I spent the next couple of years being trained in all kinds of techniques and worked on some small assignments which went well. I was reliable – and pliable.

I didn't let my own personal morals or feelings get in the way of my job – it can only work if you make a decision that you are on the side of the British Secret Service and that overrides all other considerations – if you cannot overcome your own feelings or compromise your morals, you cannot be of any use to the service. It just wouldn't work that way – the same as if all soldiers in the army were asked their opinion before every decision was made by the captain – it would get the whole platoon wiped out in a war setting. Those whose job it is to make decisions will make the decisions and those below them in the pecking order are mere operatives – they are machines who are operated by those who decide – just like the military."

"I can see how that would make sense"

"I was an operative and I operated. The jobs they gave me – and I cannot go into details for obvious reasons – took me all over the world. I loved it."

"A childhood fantasy come true"

"Exactly. After about five years I was asked if I would like to take on a very deep cover operation which would involve danger and possibly force me to kill enemies of the country – that's exactly how they worded it. I didn't hesitate – after all, soldiers kill their enemies so it wasn't very different".

"I suppose not".

"The codename for this deep cover operation was 'G10'. It has been running for a number of years. Its mission is to infiltrate a major international drug syndicate and kill as many of the high-ups in the organisation as possible"

Kill? – not arrest?" I queried.

"What's the point in arresting them? – they have very expensive lawyers – they'd be back out in minutes flat. The evidence may not be sufficient to win a court case – it's better all round if we just eliminate them. Don't forget it's a war we are fighting against drugs – and the casualties are innocent kids who get hooked on the filth they peddle"

"You don't have to justify yourself to me Johnny – I hate drugs and I despise those evil bastards who deal in them – so I've no problem with you disposing of the scum who make millions by destroying young people's lives – no problem at all"

"Well anyway I had to get involved with the drug cartel – that's how it works – unless you convince them that you are as evil as they are, they won't take you into their confidence. They always test people who join their

129

organisation. Usually, you have to commit some serious crimes or kill someone – then they have something on you if you ever turn out to be a grass"

"So, you have to become one of them – not just pretend?" I felt a bit of tension in the back of my neck and lit up another cigarette to make it go away.

"There's no other way to get deep into the syndicate. I won't go into details but over the past nine years I convinced the big dogs that I was someone they could trust in any situation. I became a big player in the organisation – I knew who most of the high up people were but not those at the very top – until recently".

"So now you know who all of them are?"

"I think so – it's always possible that I have missed a few but I know enough to smash the organisation completely – and I have a plan to".

"Sounds like you've done a good job".

"It's gone quite well" he said. There was no pleasure in his voice – no doubt he had been forced to do things that were against his morals on many occasions to get to this point. I could see in his face that the years of undercover work had taken their toll on him.

"So how come I got dragged into it?" This is what I wanted to know most of all.

"You dragged yourself into it, you nutter!" he laughed out loud as he shouted this out.

"What do you mean?" I thought I already knew what he was going to say and I was not disappointed.

"You were supposed to discover my corpse and just phone the police – I needed certain people to think I was out of the picture – to keep the integrity of my cover when the assassinations of the members of the cartel began in earnest. Instead, you went on the run and got half the police in Britain searching for you. This actually helped me – but it got you noticed by certain people"

"You can say that again!" I barked.

"The publicity created by your actions reinforced the idea that I was dead – the syndicate believed it"

"That sounds all well and dandy but why put the shotgun in my van? If I'd gone to the police and they had found it, I would have been suspect number one – and also of interest to your drug buddies – I was bound to be deep in the shit!"

"Yeah, well you can thank Mark Hopkins for that little twist. He was one of my underlings in the drug business. I'd told him I needed to fake my death to avoid an investigation by MI5 – I said I had an insider on the payroll – by the name of Glaze – who had tipped me off about a major move in my direction by the British authorities. You know what Mark is like – or should I say *was* like – couldn't resist being a smartarse or a bastard. He thought it would be a good joke to put the murder weapon in your truck. Even so, it wouldn't have taken the police more than a week or so to find out that you had no connection to the gun or to anything else linked to my shooting. I could have got a message to the powers that be telling them you were just a stooge"

"I was certainly a stooge – and a mug – and an idiot. Everybody's fool, that's Mike Garvie" I sounded as bitter as I felt.

"You only got into real danger when you called Mark Hopkins and asked him to help you hide from the police – he must have pissed himself laughing at the irony of that one!"

"I thought you said he was one of your men?"

131

"He was, but Mark was always too ambitious – he saw my 'death' as an opportunity to move up in the rankings. The fact that he knew I was actually still alive gave him some leverage over me. If I intervened in an obvious way to oppose his actions, he could let people know I was still alive – this would get them very suspicious and a lot of them would disappear into the ether overnight".

"A tricky situation". I said this because I wanted to be part of the conversation. I hate listening too long. Ask my schoolteachers.

"To cut a long story short I got onto Glaze and he made it a priority to capture or kill Mark Hopkins – take him out of the picture. We eventually got him in France".

"Did he spill the beans about you being alive during this time? I would be surprised if he didn't capitalise on this highly useful information."

"He didn't get a chance – we got hold of him as soon as he arrived in France. We let the press – and anyone else with an interest in him – think he was on the run, but he was in a special high security detention facility which we controlled and almost nobody knew about. We made him an offer during that time – to join G10 and eliminate his contacts with impunity. He jumped at the chance. He got to do what he was hoping to do anyway – move up in the organisation - and he had the British Secret Service helping him with men, equipment and weapons – all tied up with a nice free pardon wrapped in a pretty pink bow".

"At the same time, I was being drawn into G10 too – why was I needed? – I don't get it."

"That was a condition of Mark's – he wanted you involved – seems he had enjoyed toying with you so much he wanted to do it some more, his sadistic streak was an overriding personality trait – he also knew that you were an old friend of mine so maybe that was something to do with it too. It may sound crazy but I actually think Mark Hopkins liked you – felt he wanted to impress you in some way – I'm not a psychiatrist so don't ask me to explain it.".

"And you agreed to this?"

"Yes, but we insisted that you were not to be involved directly in the killings of the cartel members"

"That's nice of you"

"The Intelligence Services approached you regarding your involvement in G10 after we had agreed with Mark's demand – that's when we gave you some basic training and told you to be ready to move once you heard that Hopkins had been arrested. You know what happened next".

Basically, you got Hopkins to kill all the bad guys and then arranged to have him blown to bits in that warehouse in St. Malo?" He smiled at me like a parent whose child had just spoken his first word.

"You're catching on Mike"

"Go fuck yourself!" We both laughed. I felt a sense of relief – things were still weird and dangerous for me but nowhere near as weird and dangerous as they had been – if what Johnny Walsh had spent the last two hours explaining to me were true – which I still couldn't say for sure – it sounded plausible and answered most, if not all of my questions, so I would go along with him for now at least. I had no doubt that other questions would arise but my mind had taken all it could stand – information overload was making my head ache – so I suggested we have something to eat.

We went down to the galley and Johnny took charge - he turned out to be a very good cook and rustled up the best Spaghetti Bolognese I had ever eaten, in under an hour. We drank Malbec with our meal and for a while I felt a cosy sense of normality effuse my very being – or something like that.

We finished the bottle and went up to the wheelhouse where Johnny began making adjustments to some of the electronic equipment.

"I'm setting a slow course for Blighty" he said. I felt a sense of disappointment at his words. They underlined the fact that my time alone at sea, and the sense of freedom and happiness I had felt whilst far from humanity – was over.

Chapter 25

As we set out on the short journey back to England, I considered what Johnny Walsh had told me. I believed most of it was likely to be true.

I was relieved that Hopkins was gone – he had caused trouble for everyone he came into contact with, though he seemed to take a special delight in getting me involved in his activities.

Glaze – or so it seemed – had been a genuine member of the Intelligence Service – his job had been to oversee Hopkins and the others during those last G10 actions – he had died in the line of duty. I couldn't help wondering if he knew that the shootout in the St. Malo warehouse would end in a bomb going off to kill Hopkins. He may have been killed in the shoot-out and dead before he could make his escape from the explosion. I would probably never know this. The possibility that he had been sacrificed by his superiors as collateral damage remained a strong one in my mind. They may be the good guys but they were every bit as ruthless as the bad guys. I would do well to remember this.

I still had been given no reason why I was still needed by Walsh on this mission of his – I had no special skills or knowledge and was no soldier. I wasn't even a particularly good sailor – there were many better equipped than I was. When I brought up the subject again later that night, Johnny once more changed the subject.

I did find out why Tony Smith had been killed in such a way and at that particular time – at least Walsh gave me his theory on the subject. Johnny reckoned that somebody higher up the food chain and part of the drug cartel had found out that he was alive and that his death had been faked – this was possible – Hopkins had known and he was not one to miss out on an opportunity to benefit from inside information that good. It was also possible that someone else knew and had passed it on to the syndicate.

The killing of Tony Smith would have been their twisted way of letting Johnny Walsh know they were aware that he had faked his murder – and by killing a person so close to me – a 'friend' of Johnny's who was also involved in recent happenings, - they were showing how easy it would be for them to take me out of the picture. This theory sounded plausible if not entirely convincing.

When I decided to get away from the scene by going out on *Valerie II*, Walsh had tracked me every step of the way – there was hidden monitoring equipment installed on my boat, which enabled Johnny to keep an eye on me and attempt to keep me out of danger. That they were tracking me was evident from the fact that my boat had been fixed in Germany and shipped back to Dover in England. He told me I had needed a holiday and how pleased he had been when I had shown initiative and taken his Red Boat on an extended vacation. That boat was also tracked – even more so – as well as being controllable from wherever Johnny Walsh had been stationed during my summer break.

As we neared the south coast of England and the white cliffs of Dover came into view a few miles off, I asked Johnny what was in store for us – I had begun to think in terms of 'us', though I didn't like how it felt. For his part, Johnny had been cheerful and seemed to enjoy the journey. I still found it hard to accept – even in the

136

face of so much evidence – that this Johnny Walsh, the person I had known since childhood and who again seemed so happy and uncomplicated – was behind a complex web of deceit, murder, drugs, espionage and general mayhem.

I got no satisfactory answer regarding our immediate future – though I was told there was only one more move in the chess game and we would soon have the pieces in place to bring about a 'super-sized check mate'.

As we pulled into the marina at Dover, I saw *Valerie II* moored and looking better than I had ever seen her. I smiled as we approached and parked the Red Boat alongside her.

"I hope you like what we've done with the boat" quipped Johnny. I nodded.

"She looks amazing. Thank you for rescuing her and looking after her so well, I really appreciate it". I did appreciate it too – I would have had difficulties getting her ship shape at the harbour in Norden – my funds were not great and I knew nobody in that area who could have helped me.

"Once we've done one last little job you can sail off into the sunset and forget all this horrid business". Was that a glimpse of humanity from this big tough spy? I would reserve judgement until I knew just exactly what this 'one last little job' entailed.

I glanced up across the harbour and saw the hills behind it. There on the left of my view I saw the White Cliffs pub – a reminder of so much that had happened. I couldn't help wondering who ran the pub now – was it still linked to smuggling? or just a regular tourist pub run by a decent landlord.

"Oy, stop daydreaming and follow me, Mike!" yelled Walsh, laughing. I followed him onto the jetty and we soon reached the main car park of the marina. He led the way toward a dark-coloured Volvo and pressed a button on the key fob which unlocked the doors. "Get in!" he barked. I deliberately dithered about before doing as he ordered – I didn't like to be bossed around.

Once we were out of the boatyard and on the main road, he put his foot down and we wasted no time in getting on the motorway towards London.

We took less than two hours to cover the 160 miles to Whitehall and parked in an underground carpark beneath an unmarked building. I had no doubt this was some part of the labyrinthine catacombs in which the British Secret Service did its dirty business.

I followed Agent Walsh along several faceless corridors. We passed through a couple of heavily reinforced doorways protected by armed soldiers. We then entered a large room with no windows. There were a few hard chairs arranged in a rough semi-circle and a desk at the front with a similar chair next to it. Johnny took a seat facing the front. I sat next to him.

A tall man dressed in a smart – and very formal – army dress uniform swaggered out from somewhere and stood next to the desk. He wasted no time, introducing himself to me as General Willings – Intelligence Corps. I shook his hand – his grip was very strong.

"OK ladies – pay attention!" he commanded. I smirked. He might look like a stuffed shirt but the guy obviously had a sense of humour hidden under his bluff exterior. "I want to introduce you to the third member of your team and I suggest you brace yourself for a bit of a surprise". Johnny and I looked at each other. I made a faux-surprised face – he shrugged like he already knew who it was. A man walked out from the same somewhere as the general had come from. It was Liam Harries. A very different Liam Harries. This one portrayed none of the defeated, unhappy characteristics of the man I had spoken to in Belmarsh prison so recently. This Liam Harries was dressed as an army colonel and marched in like he was parading in front of the Queen. He turned sharply and did that foot stamp thing which soldiers are so fond of, before standing to attention facing us.

"At ease Colonel!" barked the General Willings. I couldn't help but feel this bit of overacting was put on as a joke – but you never knew with the army – I suspected some of the top brass would even march around at home, shouting orders at themselves – and their wives – as they went about their homely activities – "Tea for two in the conservatory – 0-900 hours – at the double – quick march" I chuckled to myself as I imagined this, then looked at Willings who seemed to have a roguish twinkle in his eye as he caught my gaze.

Harries relaxed – the theatrics over, and pulled a chair next to the General, who had taken the one by the desk. It seemed Harries was no longer required to keep a low profile in prison. Someone high up had decided they would gain nothing useful from his deep cover – given that the new plan made the old approach obsolete. No doubt he was extremely relieved about this change in tactics, made by those faceless wonders who held his entire future in their hands.

"I suggest we drop the formalities and get down to business – this has been a long and difficult operation and I'm sure I'm not the only one who will be extremely pleased when this mission is complete".

139

"You can say that again" quipped Johnny.

"Thank You Colonel Walsh – that's enough from you lad!" barked General Willings – I was seeing military banter at its most subtle today.

"Colonel Walsh?" I exclaimed, loudly. Johnny burst out laughing at this – Willings, likewise grinned with amusement at my surprise – he had told me to brace myself after all. Johnny stood up and held out his hand for me to shake.

"Colonel Jonathan Andrew Walsh – British Army Intelligence Corps – at your service!" he said in his best parade ground voice.

- "Well, I'll be" –

- "You already have been Mate!" Johnny replied, laughing out loud. Even Harries managed a smile at this. Seems I was the butt of a very entertaining joke – at least it was a joke to them. I rolled my eyes and shrugged – let them have their little giggle, I didn't care. In fact, I felt good about it. I had finally got real proof of where I stood and who I was being manipulated by – it was a relief to know I was only a pawn of the British Army Intelligence Corps – and not a band of cut-throat drug dealers. It felt like promotion. Harries spoke again.

"We needed someone on the outside – someone who could be trusted – if the operation went tits up and we all ended up brown bread. We felt that you would be able to offer some useful information to the intelligence services about some of the things which had occurred and a number of the people involved. When you decided to do a runner after Colonel Walsh's faked murder and went to Mark Hopkins of all people for help – we decided to let you run with it in the hope you would lead us to new information or members of the drug syndicate – or that your blundering and unpredictable actions might cause some of the gang to make sudden moves – ill-thought-out moves – which would give us opportunities to gather information on their activities and personnel"

"It sounds so nice when you put it like that!" a replied as sarcastically as I could amid a growing sense of shock. I really had been everybody's plaything – from beginning to end. I felt a fleeting sense of genuine shame for a second – but managed to push it aside with my increasing anger.

"Sorry and all that Old Chap" chimed in General Willings "Need to know and all that!" I fumed and smouldered. The next person who spoke that phrase at me was going to get my fist in his face – and bugger the consequences.

"We tried to keep an eye on you as best we could – you were followed and monitored for most of the time – we didn't want you getting killed or anything" –

"Well, I was almost killed a few times – so you didn't do a very good job did you?" I couldn't help blurting this out – it was the way these military types spoke of everything in such a detached and abstract way – I was just another asset to them and I hadn't even agreed to be one – so I was feeling extremely resentful about it.

"These things always carry a large element of risk Old Lad – can't be helped I'm afraid"

"Thanks for that general – I appreciate your genuine concern!" The general ignored my spiteful outburst.

"If it's any consolation Mr Garvie your activities did in fact help us significantly – Hopkins for one acted in ways he had not done before once you became involved. He seemed to take a special delight in messing with you and it is possible that he moved earlier in his attempt to rise in the drug trade to impress you – which was very out of character for him previously"

"Probably had a crush on me!" I was still acting like a spoilt child and I knew it but my emotions had been pent up and now they were bursting out all over the place. The army boys would just have to suck it up. Bollocks to the lot of them.

"Let's just say you had a useful effect on him which helped us move forward!"

"Yes, let's!" I sulked.

Johnny Walsh stood up and addressed the General. "I think this might be a good juncture at which to clarify the operation going forward Sir"

"Quite right Old Boy! Would you like to outline the final phase of Operation G10?"

"Nothing would give me greater pleasure Sir" replied Colonel Walsh.

I braced myself for more shocking revelations – I was not disappointed.

Chapter 26

The Red Boat pulled out of Dover and picked up speed as we entered the English Channel for the last time. This craft would not be coming back this way again. There was a very high probability that none of the crew – which consisted of myself, Harries and Walsh – would be coming back either.

The final phase of the mission was beyond crazy – it was more like suicide. On the plus side, I had been made a Captain in the Army Intelligence Corps – so my corpse – or any parts of it which could be found, would be buried with full military honours.

I had listened with ever-increasing disbelief and horror, as the final mission, the endgame, of the G10 project had been explained in shocking detail by Colonel Harries.

Colonel Walsh seemed unsurprised – I had the distinct impression that the plan was his. He had been the executive commander of the operation from the start and had pulled all our strings with expert dexterity.

Captain Garvie sat dumbfounded as he listened to the military briefing described in minute detail. I was to be an integral part of the operation and it had been made clear that if any one of us failed in our task – then the whole mission – and the entire G10 operation stretching back over a decade – would crumble to dust.

We were in low spirits as we moved out of the Strait of Dover and into the lower reaches of the North Sea.

Although we could not see them, we knew that there were eyes on us. The entire British Military was watching us on radar and there were tracking devices onboard, along with microphones and everything possible, to ensure that if we needed intense backup, we would not have to wait too long for it to arrive.

We would absolutely be requiring backup – it was integral to our plan – or our escape at any rate. If the cavalry was late, or for some reason failed to arrive at all, we were buggered. Shit or Bust didn't begin to cover it this time.

The next 24 hours were tense aboard ship. We were all too keyed up and aware of the seriousness of our mission to partake of any of the usual banter. We also had a terrible concern that we might have to fight the Norwegian Navy if the diplomatic side of the mission failed.

We were heading back to Henningsvær in Norway – the little fishing and holiday village, situated on a pretty little island off the coast of Norway. This was the place where I first encountered the amazing Red Boat. I wondered at the time why it was moored so far from the main thrust of civilisation. Now I knew – and the reasons were awful.

Firstly, it was important for the locals – and any other visitors to the harbour - to become accustomed to seeing the boat moored quietly in its position in the midst of the small bustling tourist town. Nobody would be alarmed if the boat was seen slowly approaching its usual docking bay.

If people got used to seeing the boat, then it would become insignificant – nobody was likely to take any notice of it or feel threatened by it. The people we specifically did not want to feel threatened by its presence were the twelve top members of the international drug

144

syndicate, who were known to have held meetings in a hotel in this little village on a very infrequent basis.

The clever people in British Intelligence had come up with the idea that if they could cause enough aggravation and damage to the drug operation – wiping out a few of their middle ranking managers for example; blowing up a distribution warehouse in St. Malo; if we could get hold of a few of their key men on the ground – Mark Hopkins for example – people who knew enough to start giving dangerous information regarding the higher echelons of the crime organisation; if there was a rogue civilian mixed up in it who was likely to throw a massive spanner in the works – an unknown quantity acting on emotion and impulse - then they might decide that things had got dangerous enough to call a meeting of their leaders to discuss ways of cutting off the danger and re-establishing control over the broken bits of their operation.

The Intelligence Service had received information from a deep undercover agent close to the top of the cartel that such a meeting had been called – and it was to be in a hotel in Henningsvær.

Our mission was to take the Red Boat back to its usual mooring, quietly and unspectacularly - then 'get the Hell out of Dodge' before the whole place went up in a massive explosion – wiping the top dozen leaders of the cartel off the face of the earth – the whole drug running operation would be damaged to a fatal degree. It would take years, if not decades, to build another organisation approaching the reach and power of the one we had been working to destroy for over ten years.

The Red Boat was key to the entire operation. Because the Red Boat was a floating bomb – an atomic floating bomb!

Chapter 27

We sailed into the harbour at night – the place was quiet, apart from a few very late revellers who were singing their way back to their hotels from the last bar to close.

We had been contacted by General Willings a few hours before. He informed us that the Norwegians had – extremely reluctantly, and only after a massive sum of compensation had been agreed – sanctioned the operation. They were extremely angry and horrified that all of the citizens and visitors in Henningsvær – in fact the entire village itself and everything else within a fifty-mile radius - would be decimated or polluted beyond use.

The bomb was deep in the keel of the boat – it was behind that heavy yellow door I had found – the one with what I now knew to be nuclear symbols on it. I had taken a holiday on a nuclear weapon and never even knew it!

The plan was for us to get out of Norway as soon as possible – the explosion would be detonated remotely once we had given the signal that we were clear of the area – or in two days' time at midnight – whichever came soonest. If we somehow got delayed, we would go up with the rest of the island, simple as that.

We spent that night sleeping on the Red Boat. Personally, I slept much better than I had for as long as I can remember, which was odd considering the mission we were on. I had expected nightmares about nuclear bombs going off, people running and screaming as radioactive fire and flame raced across the desolate landscape – but it seemed my subconscious was taking some time off.

I awoke around 8am and went into the galley to make myself a ham roll. Harries was there stirring a cup of coffee he had just made.

"Want a cup – the kettle has just boiled?" he asked.

"Thanks" I replied "Black, two sugars"

We stood at the kitchen counter sipping our coffee, not speaking. Harries was not a talkative man at the best of times and it didn't seem appropriate to engage in small talk about the weather when we were about to massacre hundreds of people, sleeping peacefully in their beds or having coffee in the kitchen like we were.

I understood the G10 remit to destroy the leaders of the evil drug syndicate at all costs – they had ruined thousands – perhaps millions - of lives and would destroy more people every day they remained in business. So, we had to put them out of business. This part of the mission I felt to be justified – though it circumvented more laws than I cared to think about.

What I had a very uneasy feeling about was what the military called 'collateral damage' – in other words innocent people who were killed as a by-product of killing the intended targets. They were considered of not sufficient importance to miss out on an opportunity to annihilate dangerous enemies – they had been weighed on the scales of human justice and deemed a price worth paying by those who would not be paying it.

Johnny Walsh appeared just after 8.15. He had coffee and said nothing. We cleared away the breakfast things – which under the circumstances seemed pointless - the ship was going to be nothing but molecules in 36 hours' time - but old habits die hard.

148

Just after 10am we left the Red Boat to her fate. I felt sadness at the thought of what was to happen. I had spent time getting to know her and would always be grateful for the recent vacation out in the middle of the vast quiet ocean, which we had shared. Some people get attached to their cars, seadogs like me get emotional about boats.

I got a grip of myself, walked across the aft deck for the final time. I was the last to climb down onto the jetty and walk out of the small harbour, towards the centre of this beautiful Norwegian village. The houses were all painted different colours, the air was pure and clean. In a few hours the air would be nothing but a toxic mix of radiation and body parts.

We were dressed as tourists, with a penchant for mountaineering and fishing. I had allowed my beard to grow for a while now and could have been mistaken for a genuine Norwegian. Walsh looked like an off-duty mechanic – he wore overalls, which brought back memories of the car-tinkering Johnny Walsh I thought I knew for so many years. Harries tried his best but his short hair and clean-shaven, professional appearance made him look more like a bank clerk than a tourist. At least he hadn't worn his army uniform!

Our plan was to spend an hour or so hanging around the cafés and bars – blending in as much as possible – faceless tourists among other faceless tourists. At 1pm we would board a ferry to the mainland and then take ordinary public transport – buses and trains – until we got to Oslo.

From there we would fly home on a regular flight. At the meeting in Whitehall, we had discussed the possibility of being collected by an RAF helicopter or plane but we didn't want to take even the smallest risk of someone spotting us being airlifted, so the 'civilian' route was chosen. We had plenty of time to get away.

Time passed slowly – I began to feel strongly that what we were doing was morally questionable at best and downright unacceptable at worst. I said nothing to my two associates. The fact that nobody – not even Johnny Walsh – who was usually so cheerful and bubbly – was indulging in conversation, indicated to me that they might be feeling the same.

I had no real way of knowing how they might react if I brought the subject up, so I drank coffee in cafes and pretended to be looking at the sights, just like the other visitors to this idyllic Norwegian village.

When the time came for us to get on the ferry, I walked behind the others, wondering if I would find the moral courage to at least bring up the subject of alternative courses of action. There must be another option.

At the ticket office I thought of something. I couldn't just bring it up in the ticket queue, so I waited until we were on the ferry. It would not leave for another quarter of an hour. We went up to the main passenger deck and bought coffees in plastic cups. The hot liquid tasted as sour as I felt. I took a deep breath…

"- Don't you think it's possible" –

"-NO, it's not, forget it" interjected Colonel Harries "We've thought it through about a million times in a million ways and this is the only approach by which we can guarantee all the top members of the syndicate and their aides will be eliminated. Their operation will be dead. Millions of kids will have to get hooked on drugs some other way. It will take years to build another network like this cartel has in place – the world drug trade will take a massive hit – the biggest hit ever. We will mop up almost all of the medium and small fry – the dealers, pushers, distributors, growers – it's all planned – there are a lot of people involved in this operation Garvie and they have spent over ten years putting this together. These top syndicate people almost never congregate in the same place – we don't even know who a lot of them are – we just know that whoever they are, they will be here for three days. This is the only opportunity we may ever have to destroy the entire operation in one go like this – and yes, it is absolutely horrific and disgusting that a large number of innocent people will die horribly today – but it's going to happen. You don't have to like it – I don't fucking like it – it makes me feel sick to the pit of my stomach – but it must – and will – go ahead".

I almost staggered back from the power of this verbal onslaught. I was dumbfounded.

"Colonel Harries is right Mike" said Johnny Walsh in a voice which was meant to be soothing but was just quiet – like he could hardly bring himself to say the words. "It's not something we dreamed up in the pub and scribbled out on the back of a fag packet – this comes from the very top".

"Yeah, I hear what you're saying – I guess I just have not had as long to get used to the idea as you two"

"We haven't gotten used to it – maybe accepted it as inevitable, that's all" said Harries – his voice back to its normal tone.

I lit up a cigarette and sipped my coffee. Both tasted horrible. An alarm went off as a signal that the ferry was about to move off into the sea. This was my last chance to make things different. I did nothing. I felt like a mass murderer.

Chapter 28

By the time we boarded our plane at Oslo International Airport I was feeling less bad. I always feel less when I am drunk – and now I was what in polite society might be termed 'pie eyed' or in less polite society, 'completely shit-faced'.

The plane ride passed by without me noticing it. As we disembarked at Gatwick, I had become a little more sober – but not in a good way. I had a headache and a guilty conscience to contend with.

My companions didn't look much better than I felt. The conversation on the plane had been minimal and we bid each other goodbye as we went our separate ways, after retrieving our bags from the carousel, with an air of despondency and a promise to see each other at the next briefing in Whitehall, of which, we would be notified in due course.

When I got back to Norfolk, I was extremely tired, aching and mentally jaded. I went straight to bed as soon as I got home. A deep sense of doom accompanied my dreams and I dreaded the approaching moment when I started hearing reports about a devastating nuclear attack in Norway.

My sleep was intermittent and troubled – I sensed dark shapes buffeting my body, black stringy fingers grasping inside my mind. When I awoke – bathed in sweat, with a dry mouth and throbbing head – it was still only 6 o'clock – but that was enough for me. I crawled into the shower, soaked myself in cold water, having neglected to put the boiler on to heat when I arrived the night before.

I dripped water into the kitchen, put the kettle on – a strong sweet coffee would help me function better. There was no food in the fridge. I didn't really feel like getting things out of the freezer so I drank coffee and tried to talk myself out of switching on the television.

Eventually I decided that the reality of the situation could no longer be avoided and clicked the button on the remote control.

The tv was tuned to a news channel and there was a 'breaking news' bar running across the top of the screen. A female reporter was holding a microphone and talking about an 'operation'.

She went on to explain how the British Military Intelligence Services – with help from the Norwegian authorities – had captured all twelve top members of an 'international drug ring' through a massive undercover action which involved making the aforementioned drug lords believe that a nuclear bomb was about to blow them to smithereens. They had jumped aboard several chinook helicopters they had called up to rescue them once the fact of the bomb had been leaked by a double agent - a very deep cover British agent. The choppers had been filled with heavily armed soldiers and all members of the criminal gang had been taken to a secret maximum-security facility somewhere off the coast of the UK.

No atomic bomb had been set off. No innocent people in Norway had been killed. I was not guilty of mass murder.

I cheered out loud, skipped around my sitting room, waving my arms in the air.

"I guess it was a 'need to know' basis!" I shouted. I could see now just how clever the whole operation had been. The G10 ruse had worked. After the mass killings

154

of several layers of the crime syndicate by Mark Hopkins and co – especially the big shoot-out in St. Malo – the people at the top had sensed real danger to themselves and a threat to their entire operation. This was the only reason they would ever have all agreed to meet in one place. They knew that G10 had full authority to massacre an unlimited number of their associates and would soon be getting names and addresses of the higher echelons of their organisation, from people desperate to save their own skins.

When the 'leaker' let it be known that an atomic bomb had been planted on a ship, moored just yards from their hotel – they wasted no time in getting emergency rescue helicopters sent out to them. The fact that the helicopters had been laid on by the British Military and that they had been lied to about an atomic bomb must have made them rather cross – but it was far too late to do anything about it. They were finished and they knew it.

All their fancy lawyers and paid officials would be unable to help them – British Intelligence would have moles and double agents infiltrated into every sphere of their operation – there would be no loose ends to untie or loopholes to wriggle out of this time.

I spent the next hour watching the story unfold on television. Not all the facts were in yet but that didn't stop the press from speculating. Not only were the top men who ran the crime organisation in custody, but there had also been several high-level arrests of people within the British political and military establishment – people who had been working in secret for the drug lords.

Two members of the cabinet were shipped off for interrogation – as were several members of the Intelligence Service itself.

The mission – codenamed 'G10' – had been running for over ten years. There was a solid wall of secrecy even now concerning who precisely had set up the operation – and it was still unknown – even to most people in the Secret Service – what exactly were the powers and remit of G10. One thing was clear though – G10 had been successful – it had infiltrated the infiltrators and disrupted the disruptors.

The media showed footage of helicopters taking off, landing and flying around. There were images of fast speedboats racing across lakes, cars pulling up outside hotels and men jumping out. A veritable montage of action and excitement – most of which was not related to what actually happened in any way. Since when did the press let little things like facts and accuracy get in the way of a good story?

I lazed around the house all day – eating what I could find and drinking too much rum. I slept most of the afternoon, got up around 6pm in order to attempt to make some plans for the future – I was fed up with the way I had been drifting, dragged around by fate for too long.

I would get away on *Valerie II* as soon as any debriefing meetings were over with. I expected to get a call from someone in Whitehall before long – no doubt I would be expected to give many boring statements and receive the official interpretation of everything that had happened from the moment I discovered Johnny Walsh's body five years ago – it would be tedious and not pleasant to re-live all those horrific and deadly moments I had

156

endured since I had inadvertently stumbled into this tangled web of murder and mayhem.

I was now a Captain in Military Intelligence – though I don't know if this was a temporary commission just so I was not outside the law – and the control - of the intelligence services, should things not go to plan at any time. I hoped to be released from this burden – all I wanted was to be free of it all.

I had last seen my boat, moored in Dover – looking better than she had ever looked. I had to hand it to Johnny Walsh. If there was nothing else I should be grateful to him for, it was the saving of my boat and its rescue from that German harbour. It was time to bring my boat home.

The next morning, I drove into Norwich, leaving my Land Rover at the railway station. I took the 9.03 train to Dover and after a change at Stratford, I arrived in Dover at 12.41

I got a taxi to the harbour and by 2pm I had thoroughly checked out my boat. *Valerie II* was indeed in tip top condition – she had been refuelled and anything damaged in the storm was now fixed. Johnny Walsh had made sure my boat was safe and as good as new. I bought a few provisions for the journey, set off towards the Norfolk coast at around 2.30pm.

As we moved slowly out into the Strait of Dover, I breathed a sigh of relief. I hoped this really would be a new beginning – or at least the beginning of a beginning. Once the military business was finally over, I would spend as much time out at sea as I could. I would savour the peace and quiet of my own company – and the companionship of the birds, fishes and other sea creatures.

The sea herself was indeed like a big beast, moving and growling – sometimes playful, sometimes sleepy and occasionally fierce and deadly.

A force 3 crosswind buffeted us as we moved further out – the shipping forecast had hinted that a slightly choppy passage was likely but it would only make the sailing more enjoyable – a bit of spume in the face would be refreshing to me.

I set course North-Easterly and switched on the auto pilot. Going below, I soon had a delicious meal set out on the lounge table. Ham rolls, a small pre-packed salad from the supermarket and a can of lager. I took time to enjoy my meal and felt better for it.

I washed up, put things away before going back onto the main deck to watch the ocean. I took a bottle of Captain Morgan Spiced and a glass with me and sat gazing out to sea as I sipped a well-earned libation.

It got dark slowly as we passed the Suffolk coast on our port side and approached Norfolk. I had decided to moor for the night at Great Yarmouth – it would not be pleasant trying to navigate the narrow twists and turns of the River Bure in the dark – I would take *Valerie II* back to her old berth in Tony Smith's boatyard – it would not be the same without Tony – maybe it would have closed down. I hoped I would be able to stay there for a couple of weeks at least – until I could get any outstanding legal matters finalised and hopefully, resign from the G10 operation – and the Intelligence Service – once and for all.

I had decided to put my little hideaway cottage on the market – I would live on my boat from now on – I wanted no ties or permanent links to any place or person

– I would live as a drifter on the seven seas and never be heard of, or thought about, by anyone again.

I guided the craft into a berth in Yarmouth harbour around 11.30 and was all battened down and securely locked into my boat before midnight. I even dared hope that this would be a genuine fresh start for me. Another one.

Chapter 29

I slept late – it was almost noon when I finally crawled out of my bunk, slunk down to the galley to make coffee. I got underway around 1pm, carefully navigated the twists and turns – some extremely narrow – of the River Bure, as it wound its way towards Wroxham and then on to the boatyard which had until recently been run by Tony Smith.

As I approached my old mooring position, I could see that things had changed. There was a brand new – modern metal-sided building standing in the place of Tony's old wooden one. The large sign on the side of the new warehouse named it as 'G10 Engineering'.

I felt dizzy, had to grip hold of the wheel to steady myself as I pulled in alongside the bank – just outside the new compound which had sprung up so quickly. It looked las if the right to moor here had been discontinued – there was a barrier across the entrance to the wharf and only one boat berthed inside the barrier. A large Red Boat.

How they had managed to get it here was beyond my comprehension – I had enough trouble squeezing my own boat through some of the narrows of the river on my way here. The Red Boat was a lot wider and longer than *Valerie II*. Maybe they had transported her by road – though it would surely be impossible to find a truck big enough to carry the craft and also be able to navigate the narrow roads around Wroxham.

And then I noticed something which explained what I was looking at. It was a full-sized mock up – a model – made from MDF or cardboard – or fairy dust –

who the hell knew – but it was not a real boat. It had been built here. As I moved past the wharf I could see, as my angle of view changed, that it was not solid but flimsy – it sat too high in the water and moved with every tiny wavelet which billowed against its fake hull.

This was more of a shock than the real boat being here. Somebody had gone to a lot of trouble to construct a model of the Red Boat and put it in front of a brand new warehouse which had been built on Tony's old boatyard – and it was named G10 – this felt like I was right back at the beginning, when everyone was messing with me – it made no sense – even if they had wanted to build some sort of secret warehouse they would surely not have called it G10 – and why build the boat mock up?

I peered closely at the warehouse – as close as I could get now that the wharf was blocked off – I wanted to see if it was made of cardboard too – it looked real enough though. Whether there was anything inside was another question – I would have to wait to get the answer.

The logo and name on the side didn't mean there was anything in the building – it could just be another mock-up which was put here to unsettle me – though why someone would want to go to such lengths was beyond me. Why else would this have been done right next to my little cottage?

I pulled *Valerie II* into the bank, tied her up to a couple of trees. This would have to do as a temporary mooring. If any other boats came along and wanted to get past, they would have to let me know. The river was narrow here and unless the boat was small it would not be possible to go by without scraping the paintwork.

I disembarked, made my way to the back door of my home. Everything looked as I had left it – quiet and deserted was the norm in these parts.

I let myself in, quickly searched my cottage – I felt sure there would be something unpleasant waiting inside for me. I took no more than five minutes to check all rooms, cupboards and even under my bed. As far as I could tell nobody had been inside since I last was here – there was a thin layer of dust on many surfaces, everything was in the same position and condition as when I had so recently left it.

I put the kettle on, made myself a strong cup of tea. There was a tin of chicken soup in the cupboard which I heated in a small pan and poured into a large mug.

I sat on the sofa, imbibed my comestibles, before turning on the television to catch the early evening news.

There was new information concerning the events in Norway. A government spokesman had updated the press regarding the mopping up operation, which came after the main arrests of the drug cartel leaders.

Over two hundred people - based in countries throughout the world – but mainly based in Britain, France and America – had been arrested in various police raids and were now in custody. Many of the people involved were high ranking officials, in political and military positions in the United Kingdom. Links had been found to influential departments of Special Branch, MI5 and the Metropolitan Police.

The newsreader informed the viewers that large numbers of people who had been employed to keep drugs off the streets and out of the country, had in fact been working to do the exact opposite. These double agents had now been replaced by people who would supposedly work to "keep the country safe from the evil of drug trafficking".

There was no mention of G10 by name – nor did the names of Harries, Walsh or Garvie appear in the news bulletin.

I slept with one eye open that night. The presence of the Red Boat mock-up and the big G10 warehouse just yards from my home made me feel decidedly uneasy.

In the morning I slunk out of my front door, sneaked down the muddy track, to the village shop. It always opened early – farmers and country bumpkins are not known for lazing around in bed till eight o'clock like townies do.

Mrs Bolton was placing some magazines into a wall mounted wire rack when she heard me come in. She immediately sprang into action. Her gossip levels were obviously full to bursting.

"Ah, Hello Mr. Garvie – and how are things with you this morning?" she enquired. I shrugged.

"Well to tell you the truth Mrs. Bolton things are a bit odd in my cosy corner – there seems to be a massive warehouse where Tony's boathouse used to be – I don't suppose you know anything about that do you?" She was delighted at my question.

"Yesterday morning they cut through from the woods behind Tony's wharf – looked like army to me – they've ruined the woods out on the Wroxham side – cut a massive track through to the boatyard. Blocked the traffic for over three hours – it was absolute chaos".

"I saw the warehouse last night when I brought my boat back from Yarmouth – I must admit I was surprised how things had changed". I spoke in a calm –

almost jovial manner – like it meant nothing to me other than an intriguing bit of local gossip.

"You can't moor in the wharf anymore – they've blocked that off too"

"Yeah, I noticed – I had to leave my boat moored up to the bank – I'm blocking the river but I had no choice – I don't suppose there will be many boats coming this way if the wharf has gone and Tony too. There's not even room to turn my boat around – I'm going to have to keep on up to the wider stretch by Tanner's Farm before I can turn round". Mrs. Bolton grimaced in sympathy with my predicament.

"It's all a bit odd if you ask me" she said.

"You can say that again" I agreed. I picked up a wire basket and began putting a few tins of soup, some ham, and other provisions into it. She hovered behind me.

"I don't suppose you would know anything about what's going on would you Mr. Garvie?"

"Sorry Mrs. Bolton – I've been away a lot lately – boat trips and that sort of thing – so I can't help you at all I'm afraid".

"Oh well" she sounded disappointed – had hoped that I might be involved in the activities in some way – being so close to the location of the action and all that – also I was an outsider, so always likely to prove a prime suspect.

I continued to fill my basket, then went to the counter and paid – adding some cigarettes to my haul before exiting the shop, leaving Mrs. Bolton looking frustrated that she had found out nothing juicy from her interaction with me. I was likewise a little disappointed that she had not known more about the changes to the wharf area. She had contacts in the local constabulary and

164

knew at least one reporter from the local rag – maybe she knew more than she wanted to tell someone who - by Norfolk standards - was a stranger and not to be trusted.

At least I knew they had come in through the woods – the Wroxham Road had been blocked – by the army – the whole operation had been over in about three hours.

I could not see how it was possible to build an entire warehouse in three hours – three days would have been incredible – three weeks fast – three months highly efficient. Something felt decidedly iffy about the whole thing. I would have to take a closer look at this new warehouse.

I dropped my shopping off in the cottage, then walked back to the road which linked the village and the town of Wroxham – the so called 'main road'.

About half a mile along – moving away from the village – I saw what Mrs. Bolton had described - how they had ruined the woods. There was a thirty-foot-wide swathe cut out of the trees and the ground had been churned up by the movement of large vehicles.

I stealthily moved along the right side of this track – keeping close to the trees which still stood there. A few hundred yards of nothing much, then a newly fitted six-foot-high metal gate and some chain-link fencing barred my way. There was a small sign on the gate telling me it was private property. I tried the gate – it was padlocked, so I climbed over it, ran into the shadow of the new warehouse. There was a large roller door at the front which was designed to allow access to large vehicles or equipment – I had noticed a similar door at the water side of the structure – these were heavily padlocked and chained shut.

165

As I followed the side of the structure, I found a metal door on the side. I tried the handle, was only half surprised when it opened. I had already surmised that the whole set-up was for my benefit – though I had no idea why someone would go to such trouble on my behalf. I had my suspicions as to who was behind it but their motives were as obscure and quirky as ever as far as I could fathom – which wasn't far.

Inside was a lot of space and little else – the building was a shell – it was not even a building – more a giant metal box. I had a horrible feeling I would get trapped in it. I left the door open, glanced around for other escape routes should one become necessary – there were no other escape routes that I could see.

I swiftly moved towards the centre of the space, picked up a letter which had been left on the dusty floor. It was addressed to me. I tore it open. It was typed but signed in a swirly signature which said 'Johnny'.

The letter informed me that this warehouse was my reward for all the help I had given the 'Service' in my recent and not so recent escapades. The name G10 engineering was just his little joke, not to be taken seriously. I could change the company name to whatever I wanted. The land had been purchased and put in my name – the pathway through the woods was being granted the right to add a paved road – I could keep my boat here and there was a nice boating-related enterprise to be set up for me to run – marine supplies and maintenance – a bit like Tony Smith's old boatyard but a lot more modern and efficient. I could order any equipment I saw fit, the bills could be posted to a company address which would be sent to me in due course.

Basically, I was out of the service, this was to be my golden handshake. It would have been nice to have been asked if I wanted to run a business - somebody had decided I did - and that was that – it was more of the same as far as these shadowy authorities were concerned – they told you who to be and what to do and you just did it. It really pissed me off. I was not going to be a pawn in their new game – even if that game might have certain attractions, like a good income, an interesting career. They had toyed with me, messed with me, nearly killed me and now they wanted to pat me on the head, make me do what I was told.

It didn't feel right on any level – but then nothing had felt right since that day when I had been deliberately dragged into a maelstrom of upheaval by Johnny Walsh's fake murder. I seethed with rage, tore the letter into tiny pieces before sprinkling the floor with the remnants. I turned and stormed out of the facility – I was furious that even now they were trying to manipulate me with an arrogant certainty that I would simply fall into line like so many others no doubt had done before.

By the time I reached my cottage I was a little calmer but still annoyed. I made myself a ham sandwich, washed it down with a cup of strong black coffee. I lit up a cigarette – it seemed I was still on them part-time nowadays. I wandered up to my bedroom to grab my shaving kit. I would think more clearly after a wash and brush up.

By midday I had decided to let things slide – I would make no moves – if they wanted to play games, I would let them play them alone. If I refused to participate, they would be forced to declare more of their hand and I might be able to figure out just what they were up to – not that I had been very successful at that up until now.

Three days later a sheaf of legal papers arrived for me to sign – these papers released me from my temporary position in army intelligence, notified me that I would remain under the jurisdiction of the Official Secrets Act. I was informed that I would not need to attend any debriefing sessions in Whitehall but that they reserved the right to arrange any debriefing they deemed necessary in the future.

The Ministry of Defence had paid £25,000 into my bank account by way of '*backdated salary to cover all periods of employment*'. This did not include '*compensation for losses and hardship*' which would be assessed and paid to me at a later date.

I was also informed in writing that the option to accept the warehouse and the set-up of a marine engineering and maintenance company was time limited – I had just two weeks to sign and return the corporate documents. This offer was termed a '*performance bonus*' as it was felt by those responsible for making such awards, that I had been '*put under extreme duress and had lost my livelihood as a direct result of the work I had done on behalf of her Majesty's Government*'. The way these people liked to spin things to make them sound civilised and well-planned amazed me.

I spent a couple of boring days reading through every paragraph of the documents I had been sent. I signed the document which stated that I understood I was still subject to the official secrets act and another which spelt out my release from all sections and operations of the Secret Service and the British Military. I was now a civilian again – it was very odd to think that I was being released from positions I never even knew I held – I was surprised it was even possible that a person could be a member of the military or intelligence services without ever having been notified or agreeing to become so. I was glad to be out of this tangled shadowy loop of intrigue and double-dealing.

I was also delighted to accept the 25 grand – it was the least I felt they owed me after causing me so much stress, putting my life and sanity in danger with their psychological warfare techniques.

The offer of the warehouse and business I would ignore – allowing the offer to time-out. I did not want to run a big company – did not want to be linked in any way to these underhand, dangerous people – did not want to stay in Norfolk – or England. I wanted only one thing – to take *Valerie II* out to sea and stay there. With the funds I now had at my disposal, I was free to do exactly that.

Chapter 30

A week later, I received confirmation in writing from the Ministry of Defence – on fancy headed notepaper with official watermarks and logos all over it – that I was free to continue my life as a civilian, all links to the government departments were now legally severed.

Two weeks later I got another official document, informing me that the offer of the warehouse and business had been withdrawn due to my lack of response.

I heard not a peep from Johnny Walsh or any of the individuals I had been involved with on the operations I had participated in. I was glad of that – I wanted to forget the lot of them – to get the sour taste of corruption, murder, war, drugs, manipulation, abuse of power and general unpleasantness out of my mouth – the nausea and filth out of my gullet and guts. I felt sick to the pit of my stomach, my mind was still reeling at the events and interactions I had been forced and tricked into by these people who might be seen as the 'good guys' from a distance but were terrifying psychopaths up close and personal.

To this end, I put my cottage up for sale at a bargain price and had a buyer within a few days – it took another month for the solicitors to complete the conveyancing, the contracts to be exchanged and handover of keys to be completed.

The house sale got me another £100,000 so I was – by my standards at least – a very rich man. I had no ties and no objectives, other than to sail aimlessly out to sea as soon as the last loose ends were tied up – which they were within 24 hours.

I had moved my boat back to Great Yarmouth harbour a few weeks ago. On the day that the house sale money hit my account, I drove into Yarmouth and climbed aboard. My sense of relief was indescribable. I had a superb boat, enough money to live free in the world's oceans for several years if I so desired.

There was nothing I wanted more. I wasted no time. I untied *Valerie II*, slowly steered her out of the marina and into the North Sea. I turned North, moved out about a mile – following the North Norfolk coastline round as far as Cromer.

I anchored my boat, dropped my rib dinghy into the water – the outboard was soon buzzing. It took ten minutes to reach the shore – I left my little craft among the crab fishermen's boats on a little slipway just along from the pier.

I spent a couple of hours walking along the cliff top, enjoying the view of the sea and the flower-filled gardens which line the cliff top. After buying the best fish and chip dinner in the area – Mary Jane's is always busy and rightly so – I strolled round the small town, popped into the local supermarket for a few necessaries – milk, bread, rum, ham, some fresh tomatoes – before going back to my dinghy.

I chatted to a couple of crab men for a few minutes – mainly about expected tide and weather patterns. When they asked me where I was going, I told them I was headed precisely nowhere – just drifting where the tides wanted to take me.

Once back on-board *Valerie II,* I started her up and headed along the North Norfolk coast. I stayed close to land because I wanted to sight-see the wonders of this beautiful area. I was in Hunstanton as darkness began to

171

fall. I moored in a little private marina for a small overnight fee. The fairground on the seafront was in full swing, the little town lively and beautiful with its dark sandy cliffs spreading out each side of the centre. I stayed ashore just long enough to grab a burger from a fairground stall, stretch my legs on the promenade before going back to my boat and settling down for the night.

Overnight the sea got choppy. I didn't sleep as well as I had expected – maybe I hadn't had enough excitement or exercise – it might take a bit of getting used to – not being involved in danger and death. I was willing to sacrifice sleep for peace though, so I woke happy at 6am and got underway by 7.

Today I would leave England – perhaps forever – maybe just for a long time. I was drawn to far and distant places. Now I had the money to indulge my dreams fully, I intended to get going and not look back.

By early afternoon I was passing Skegness on my port side, heading north towards the Humber Estuary.

My plan was to slowly move up the east coast of England as far as Grimsby before turning North-West and heading North of Denmark. Here I would move into the Skagerrak strait, which ran between the Jutland peninsula, south of Norway.

This would take me into the Kattegat Sea area which in turn would let me thread my way between Danish islands, north of Germany, eventually tipping me into the Baltic. I would have to navigate some of the busiest shipping lanes in the world but this would simply add to the fun of boating.

I took my time – I was in no hurry to be anywhere in particular - I was just sailing. The wind picked up, became fairly strong as I approached the Danish coast –

which brought back memories of the storm I got caught in last time I brought *Valerie II* out this way – but the gales were not bad enough to damage my boat – only rattle a few pots and pans, spill some milk I had left out on the small table in the galley.

As I passed along the Skagerrak, I saw large container ships and a couple of rusty oil tankers, flying flags of convenience, registered in Russia and Liberia mostly. There were various smaller merchant ships popping in and out of nearby Danish and Norwegian ports. Once I had rounded the Skagen peninsular at the northern point of Danmark, I turned South-South-East into the Kattegat Sea, moved to within half a mile of the Swedish coast.

The next morning, I pulled into the large harbour at Gothenburg and spent a couple of nights exploring the bars and restaurants of the lively Swedish city. I slept on the boat at night, went sightseeing during the day and bar-crawling until late. I was wealthy by my standards and determined to live the high life. I visited the most expensive restaurants, hung out at a very exclusive night club in the city centre.

I denied myself nothing and felt better for it. I became refreshed – if a little tired - my spirits rose considerably after this break from concern and caution – I was reckless with my money and my attitude. I did not enhance the already somewhat tarnished reputation of the Great British Tourist – and I didn't give a damn. If you're on holiday, you're on holiday – not just from your normal routine but also from all the civilised behaviours the British torture themselves with under normal circumstances. Frankly I became a drunken yob. I cannot remember when I enjoyed myself more.

173

After two wild nights, I quietly slipped out of the harbour and continued on my way – thanks Sweden – it was fun!

I took two days to slowly navigate down towards Helsingborg and further half a day to reach the amazing Øresund Bridge which had recently opened – giving road and rail connections between Denmark and Sweden. It is an amazing feat of architecture. After its five miles above the water, it descends to the artificial island of Peberholm, then goes beneath this man-made island into the two and a half mile long Drogden Tunnel.

I passed the bleakly beautiful Nabben Nature reserve a few hours later before turning East into the Baltic Sea proper. I set the boat's autopilot for the Polish coast and spent a few hours catching up on some sleep.

It was during this sleep that an event happened which was to change not just my life forever, but the entire world. The Norwegian tourist town of Henningsvær was wiped off the map by a massive atomic explosion.

Chapter 31

I rose early, refreshed from my sleep, turned on the radio in the galley, while I made my breakfast. Instead of the tinny cheerful Swedish pop music I had expected, there was a man talking very earnestly about something – I could not understand the lingo, so I reset the radio to an English-speaking global news channel.

To say I was shocked by the news would be the understatement of the century. The entirety of Henningsvær had been annihilated.

When I discovered that Half of St. Malo in France and part of Dover in England had also suffered atomic explosions, I became faint, had to sit on the floor for a few minutes. My heart was pumping like a jackhammer, my beathing had become laboured.

The bombs had gone off simultaneously at around 2am GMT. Government spokespeople were making urgent statements containing no useful information and the current estimates – guesses by the media – were that somewhere between 100,000 and 500,000 people had been killed.

I staggered into the lounge, poured myself a neat shot of rum which I swallowed in one gulp. I followed this up with another. The liquor strengthened my nerves. I took a few controlled breaths. I scrambled around in a cupboard, found an old pack of cigarettes – I had not restocked, planning to give them up again – the hot toxins helped pull me together. I sat smoking with my eyes shut.

Thoughts raced around my head like a crazy whirlpool. It was clear to me that the explosion in Norway was due to the bomb on the Red Boat – it had obviously been a lie that there was no bomb. Maybe they had always planned to use the bomb if the plan to get the drug barons onto army helicopters had failed. But it had not failed and the bomb had still been detonated. I could not understand this. However, this event paled into insignificance when compared to the explosions in France and England – these had happened in highly populated areas. The radiation could make large parts of the UK and France uninhabitable for years – maybe decades. The world I knew would never be the same again.

I went up to the flying bridge, turned off my boat's engines – I needed peace. I would let her float where the tides dictated – I was miles from any land – here outside the main shipping lanes, the marine traffic was less. Several times I stood on the deck, screamed to the skies in impotent rage, confusion and fear. I saw little lights flecking before my eyes and almost fainted. I slumped to the floor, rolled around, squirming in pain which wracked my whole being. I felt my sanity slipping away along with my consciousness.

Chapter 32

I opened my eyes. Saw light blue sky. Heard gulls. I was lying on my back on the upper deck. I heard a loud noise – an alarm of some sort – it was coming from below. I scrambled to my feet, went down into the lounge area – the sound was coming from the radio room.

A red light was flashing on the binnacle. I had no idea what its significance was. I pressed some buttons but the sound continued. I picked up the radio handset, pressed the talk button. A squelching noise was heard. I released the button, set my radio to receive mode. The alarm stopped. A voice came through the communicator.

"Ahoy there, shipmate – where have you been – I've been calling for ages?" Fury on my part.

"You bastard – you set off those atom bombs – you murdering cunt!" he ignored my outrage, continued like we were having a little chin wag about the weather.

"I just wanted to let you know we are waiting for you"

"Well, you can just jolly well keep on fucking waiting bucko – you are all completely mad – you do know that don't you?"

"I can see why you might think that – not knowing all the information" there was a chuckle to his voice.

"I'm glad you find the killing of half a million people so amusing, you egotistical prick!"

I switched off my radio, threw the handset down in anger. To my amazement this had no effect. I could still hear him talking. They had obviously fitted some special upgrades to my radio when they so kindly mended my boat in Germany.

177

"Listen Garvie you need to stop having teenage tantrums and get your arse over to Riga – there will be a plane waiting for you until Tuesday at noon – after that you can forget us – things are not going to get any better for you if you stay here – there is a radiation cloud of immense proportions heading your way – and tidal waves one hundred feet high too. If you go full throttle, you might just get to the Latvian coast before you drown"

"I don't understand what's going on" was all I could say – things had moved so far out of my control and understanding that I felt helpless. Maybe if I let the tsunami drown me it would be my best option.

"Never mind that now, just get to Riga – before Tuesday noon – the plane leaves at that time whether you're on it or not"

"Where abouts in Riga?" I asked feebly.

"Don't worry, we will be monitoring your movements – we will come to get you"

"That makes me feel a whole lot better – NOT!"

"Just get there!" The radio went dead.

Chapter 33

It was around nine the next morning that my boat was capsized by a massive wave. I was about a mile off the coast of Lithuania – near a small town named Palanga. The seas had been getting rougher for a few hours and I was racing towards land when a wave - much larger than the ones I had been experiencing, hit my boat at the wrong angle and she went over, rolled like a bingo ball in a fountain.

I found myself flying through the air, then going deep under the water. I said a prayer to a God I didn't believe in. My lungs began to feel like they were going to burst as my body was thrown around by the power of the forces that had been unleashed. Part of me didn't care – it would be the end of all my problems.

Suddenly I was back on the surface – the freak wave had moved on. I was now in relatively calm seas – at least for now. I twisted around, saw behind me a long stretch of beach – about a quarter of a mile away. I knew I could swim that far and started towards it. The back current worked against me, made it a lot harder than it should have been but I managed it.

With a sense of relief, I crawled onto the sand, took five minutes to get my breath back.

I sat up and looked around me – a deserted beach behind me, rough seas in front. I saw no evidence that I ever had a boat – there was no debris floating in the water – *Valerie II* had gone down to Davy Jones' Locker – that was the end of my boating life. I had no intention of getting involved with them any longer. Most of the problems or situations – or crises – I had suffered over the past five years had been – if not caused by – at least linked to, my marine life. I would be a landlubber from now on – if I could find a piece of land to lub on, which was not in danger of becoming radioactive in the near future.

It was like a bad dream – I had spent my childhood being told we were in danger of nuclear war - it was always a thing we worried about as kids – thanks to the fearmongering of the press. After the end of the cold war, I had let this fear dissipate to nothing. Most people never even considered it a possibility these days. And now it had happened. And it was nothing to do with the Russians.

I was convinced that this atomic nightmare had been unleashed by a boy I went to school with – I could hardly accept it was possible. Johnny Walsh had destroyed Europe and who knew what other countries he would destroy next.

He obviously had help from some powerful shadowy figures linked to the British establishment but it was too crazy to contemplate, there was no way to come to terms with what had happened. It was illogical, absurd.

Yet it had happened. And here I was now on a deserted beach in Lithuania – my boat gone, my hope of a peaceful life gone, my country gone – the radiation would make the entire UK uninhabitable for decades – maybe hundreds of years. Nothing would ever be the same again. I had to stop thinking in the old ways – update my map of reality – which was impossible because I had no information regarding the nature of the new reality in which I existed.

I stood up, walked away from the water – up a sandy slope which led to some scrubby heathland and a

180

wide empty plain stretching out both sides of my viewpoint. Directly ahead I saw a few low buildings – possibly houses. I made my way slowly towards them.

I had lost all my possessions when I was thrown overboard, had just the clothes I stood up in – no money, no keys, no nothing.

Walsh had told me to get to Riga in Latvia – he had said they were monitoring me – probable he meant my boat - so now they would not know where I was – which despite the predicament I was in without their 'help', I was relieved about. I wanted nothing to do with Johnny Walsh or any of his psychopathic cronies and acolytes. I just wanted to go somewhere safe from the nuclear fallout which was heading this way. That was my only goal.

As I approached the low buildings, I could see they were small storage sheds – they looked abandoned. I tried the door of one of the two huts, it opened with a creak. The place was empty apart from a lot of grey sand and a rusty engine of some sort. The other shed had a couple of beds and some cupboards – it had been inhabited at some time, though by the amount of sand and dust in the place not for some considerable time. I searched the cupboard, found a dusty bag of brown rice which had spilled much of its contents on the shelf below. I chuckled at the thought that however bad things had got, I was not yet so desperate as to consider eating brown rice. I slammed the cupboard door, left the sheds behind me.

I looked back towards the sea – the waves were very large now – the beach was flat; the water was coming further up the sand with each inflow. There was a black cloud forming in the East. I wondered if it was atomic –

I didn't know anything about nuclear bombs – apart from the fact they contaminate whole areas. Lithuania was not so far from Norway, so it looked bad.

I ran up the beach, found a gritty track which seemed to lead nowhere in particular. In the distance I could see what looked like a small town – maybe this was Palanga – I knew I was somewhere around that area from the last location info I had seen on my boat before the shipwreck.

I followed the path, feeling completely hopeless. I had no money, no identity papers, no passport, no nothing. I was a nobody in the middle of nowhere. Maybe that's the ultimate definition of freedom!

I slowed down, walked towards the little collection of buildings I saw in the distance – maybe two miles away at a guess. There was no point hurrying – I had nowhere to get to and I was not likely to escape the radiation cloud which was heading this way.

The black cloud was now covering half the sky and it was suddenly a lot colder – the term 'nuclear winter' came to mind, though I really didn't know what it meant – it was just one of those meaningless sayings bandied about by the media, created to instil fear and sell papers.

I was past caring – or rather I had realised that caring about what happened next would be pointless, as there was no way I could know what would occur and I had no way of influencing it if I did know. I was an ant crawling across a patio – changing direction for no apparent reason, going round in circles, wasting my energy, fooling myself.

I eventually reached the town of Palanga which was almost completely deserted – news of the atomic explosions had caused nearly everyone to flee towards – who knew where?

I was living in a dystopian novel – the wind blowing debris along the street – windows broken in some shops – no people apart from a few lost souls who either didn't know what to do or just didn't care. I could appreciate their point of view.

I went into an abandoned supermarket and made myself a ham sandwich. I washed it down with a bottle of local lager which tasted like piss – and not good piss either. I then raided the cigarette counter and lit up. The brand name was in writing I could not understand and the taste was nasty.

I went over to the bank of three cash desks – the tills had already been emptied by some enterprising thief – I wished them luck. I guess no rules apply in the middle of a global disaster. It felt good to me. I was happier outside the law – my naturally non-conformist mind felt released. I realised that 'civilisation' was the biggest threat to the human race. I laughed out loud.

Somebody else laughed behind me. I turned and saw an old man. He was frail looking – his clothing was that of a fisherman or sailor. He was sipping from a half-empty bottle of what I assumed to be vodka. The old man offered the bottle to me. I wiped it on my shirt and took a swig – it was either petrol or some sort of jet fuel – I wasn't sure which. I nodded my thanks; he smiled and took the bottle back. He said something in a language I did not recognise – probably Lithuanian. I just smiled back. The man waved his hand, walked past me out of the shop – he held an amusing conversation with himself as he passed out onto the street. I shrugged.

After ten minutes searching the place, I had found some useful items and a rucksack to put them into. Mainly food, drink and cigarettes – also a couple of large, very sharp kitchen knives and some warmer clothing.

As I stepped out of the little supermarket, I almost bumped into three boys who ran by at that precise moment. They laughed, continued along the street to who knew what destination. There were not many people left in this town but it seemed that those who were still here were really enjoying themselves.

I looked along the road in the direction the boys had taken and decided that there may be a good reason why they were in such a hurry to go that way – so I walked along in the same direction.

The shops got larger – this was obviously the town centre now – some big department stores, a lot of boutiques and restaurants. Most of the places were completely deserted – some had people inside – helping themselves to the abandoned stock – though for what purpose you'd need it in the current circumstances I could not work out. The last thing I wanted was to lug around a big television as the nuclear fallout loomed.

I was approaching the main bus station – most of the buses had already left town. There were a few people hanging around for reasons of their own. Nobody took any notice of me.

I went into the bus shed at the back of the forecourt – this was probably where they fixed up any buses which broke down – there were workbenches and big tools placed around the edges of a garage area. A green bus was parked near to a rear paved area. Climbing on board I saw that the keys were in the ignition – probably it was in the process of being repaired – I hoped

184

the work had been completed as I turned the key. It fired up, the engine sounded smooth.

I whacked it in gear. The bus pulled away with only a slight jerky motion – the clutch was a little clunky but it worked – that was the main thing.

As I pulled out of the shed, saw some people running toward me – they probably wanted to go somewhere. I floored the accelerator, swished past them in a cloud of noise and blue smoke – they could catch the next one – I didn't want to get mixed up with a bunch of unknown quantities at this point – I could see no benefit to me in taking them with me – so I didn't.

The main street carried on in a straight line for about half a mile before the shops got less and the road narrowed into a wide dusty track. I had no idea where I was heading but the sense of movement made me feel I was making progress.

There was little traffic on the road – I only met one car coming back the other way and a few vehicles overtook me recklessly – desperate to get away from whatever nuclear-related fears had been activated within them by the media coverage.

I got the sense that wherever this road ended, most people were also heading in that direction – which may indicate I was headed towards a larger conurbation from which I might find a quick way of escaping the country – I was sure that any planes which might have flown from local airports would already have left – but you never knew your luck.

I carried on for over an hour – several groups of people tried to get me to give them a lift in my empty bus but I had decided to think only of myself from now on – the burden of other people's needs, suggestions and

185

influence was something I wanted nothing to do with. I no longer felt part of the human race – I was simply an object moving through a landscape. Maybe I had finally cracked up mentally – whatever the cause, I was focussed fully on saving my own arse – and as for others – bollocks to the lot of 'em!

I turned left onto a larger road – which according to road signs was the A1. This passed through quiet, deserted countryside. I could have been back in England if the scenery was anything to go by. Here I picked up speed a little – which made the problem of people trying to get on board less frequent – very few of what must now be termed refugees, were willing to try to stop a bus travelling at 60km per hour. Until a few hours ago these desperate souls were just local people living quiet country lives – just as their ancestors had done among these very fields for generations. It was hard to come to terms with the fact that people I knew – including someone I had known as a boy – could be responsible for uprooting these innocent people.

It was getting dark when the number of people walking and the tailback of traffic, got so bad that I had to slow almost to a stop. It was no longer feasible to ignore the attempts of people to get on the bus – I would have been lynched – so I reluctantly opened the double doors on the side of the bus, watched as the vehicle became crammed with far too many people.

The bus began to labour under the strain, was in imminent danger of breaking down. The traffic in front of me was moving at a snail's pace. I saw no advantage to remaining on board, so I stopped the bus and jumped off – disappearing into a crowd of humanity before anyone could stop me. It was likely there was somebody on the

186

bus who was capable of driving it – though at what speed and for how long before it conked out, I knew not.

I pushed my way to the edge of the road, saw a few buildings coming up on the left-hand side. These turned out to be offices which were – like everything else – abandoned.

I pushed my way into the first of these offices – there was a large reception area with people sitting around looking dazed. The people who worked there had left. I went up a flight of stairs to the upper floor of this two-storey building, peered out of the window.

I noticed the long stream of refugees was heading toward a large building about half a mile away – from what I could see it looked like a railway station or bus depot. I thought the chances of getting any form of public transport was minimal at best. I would head across some fields into a wooded area I had noticed far off in the distance. It would be quieter there and no less likely to sustain life than an overcrowded road.

I climbed over a low fence at the back of the office building, began walking swiftly across some open ground towards a large meadow. This meadow gave a clear path towards the woodland I sought.

The black cloud which had earlier threatened to deposit something unpleasant on my head, had now been left behind. There was a clear, watery-blue sky. The weak sun of late afternoon offered enough warmth to lift my spirits a little as I plodded across the open grassland.

I climbed over a wooden stile, into a fenced off area of forest. I followed a grassy pathway to the right – it continued along the edge of the trees, before turning a sharp right and disappearing into the dark tree-covered interior of the woods. Here the path narrowed a little, became covered in leaves and twigs. It was soft underfoot. I made good progress. I saw a wooden hut on the left and pushed the door open.

Inside was a small rickety table and chair – also an old-fashioned oil lamp hanging from a bracket. I assumed this was some sort of woodman's hut – a place for the forestry workers to rest, make tea and eat their sandwiches – it was too small to be someone's home but it offered shelter from the rain or a place to sit if the sun ever got too hot in these parts – which I thought unlikely.

I would gain nothing by remaining here, however tempting it might be. On the other hand, it was hard to see what I could gain by continuing to travel at a snail's pace across the vast landscape of this country with no particular aim in view.

I was concerned about the possibility of nuclear fallout reaching me, but had no news regarding the likelihood of this, or the related events going on in western Europe.

What I needed most was a source of English-language news, food, water and shelter. This hut was shelter only.

I had no map, compass or knowledge which could help me figure out where I was or where I should head to. I would just have to keep moving in the same direction until I found a road, then follow it. If I could avoid the mass crowds who headed for major population centres, I would have more chance of finding the things I needed – there would never be enough resources for massive crowds of people – I would be better on my own.

I had enough food and water to keep going for a couple of days. My visit to that deserted supermarket had been more fortuitous than I had realised at the time. I hoped that by aiming for smaller towns, I would find other facilities before I ran out of provisions.

I left the hut, made my way across some large fields which seemed to be growing nothing but scrubby grass and weeds. Further on I saw some smaller fields with crops growing. I walked towards these, found that the crop was wheat and therefore of no immediate use to me.

It began to get dark. I began to look for some shelter where I could sleep overnight. I needed rest, my feet were starting to hurt.

I continued through the wheat fields and was beginning to think I might have to sleep on the open ground when I saw a wire fence running along the edge of a field. I climbed through this wire fence, found myself on a narrow tarmac road. I turned right, walked up a short hill to where the landscape opened out below me, giving a good view of my location. To my left I could see a small town or village – about five miles away if my estimation was correct. The road looked as if it led there, so I moved in that direction.

A mile or so along this road, I found a stone shelter – possibly a bus shelter – went inside to have some food and a drink. I needed sleep badly and was not too eager to keep walking any longer. I was not keen on the idea of arriving in the town at night – I thought early morning would ensure minimum other people around. Night people tended to be more aggressive and unpredictable – I would take my chances with the early risers.

I settled down, slept fairly well for a few hours. When I awoke it was dark. There were a few clouds in the sky but many stars showed. I ate some bread and ham and took a few swigs of water.

I had lost my watch, had no idea of the time. It felt like the middle of the night to me, so I tried to get a bit more shut eye. I dozed a little but could not get back to sleep. I soon got frustrated with this and decided to continue my trek along the road towards the small town.

I took my time – walking very slowly in the darkness – until it started to get a little lighter. I could make out the beginnings of the settlement – I passed a few farmhouses which all looked deserted – although they had probably always looked like that at night. No dogs barked. Maybe the occupants had abandoned their homes, joined the long lines of the suffering and dispossessed trailing their way to nowhere.

As day began to break, I arrived in the centre of the town. It was large enough to have a town hall, various shops selling food, clothing and other everyday items. There were a couple of cafes and a restaurant.

The restaurant was boarded up and the supermarket looked like it had been stripped of any useful items. There were very few people around at this early hour – just lost sheep looking for basic provisions – or those unable to cope psychologically with the fact that a massive cloud of deadly dust was on its way to kill them.

I eventually found what I was looking for – a shop which sold electrical goods. While the place had been given a good going over and most of the stock had been broken or taken – I managed to find a small radio which being a display item in the store, had batteries in it.

I managed to tune it to an English-speaking news channel and didn't have to wait long to find out that most of Europe was in turmoil. Britain was in total meltdown

– society's structures had been replaced with a huge wave of chaos as people tried to escape the island by plane, boat – or some even attempting to swim the channel. The geographic protection afforded by living on an island under normal circumstances becomes a liability if you suddenly need to get off the island.

France was likewise in a state of emergency. The cloud of radioactive dust had been blown by the wind North-West – which meant that the whole of France – and parts of other nearby countries such as Holland and Belgium, had been drenched in atomic particles. As the wind picked up it had changed direction – heading due West – it was currently approaching the East coast of America and millions of people were headed West – the roads, airports and railways all clogged to a standstill.

I was relieved to hear that the nuclear fallout was not headed towards me here in Lithuania. Obviously, the wind was likely to change direction at some point but for now at least I would have a bit of breathing space – time to come up with some sort of a plan.

I was determined to get as far away from Europe as I could. Apart from its Baltic coast, Lithuania is a land-locked country, so my options would be road, rail or air. Air would be quickest but the least likely to be available – the major airports would all be jammed with thousands of people wanting to escape.

Railway stations likewise would be full – although if the trains could be kept running, there was a chance that the amount of people still trapped in the outlying stations of small towns like this one, would dissipate considerably in a few days at most. This would probably be my best option – particularly as the main roads were at a complete standstill from what I had seen.

I walked around the little town for a while, managed to find a small newsagent's shop which still had a few items worth stealing. I grabbed a couple of packets of maize snacks that had been overlooked and stuffed them into my rucksack. My water was getting low but I had enough for a day or so if I was careful.

I followed the directions on a signpost and found the railway station. There were a lot of people sleeping on the platforms, hoping a train would turn up. I estimated there were at most three train loads of people here – based on an estimation of the local trains pulling no more than three or four carriages – if by any chance a larger train could be brought here, I may even get on one by the end of the day.

This was total speculation on my part – for all I knew there would be no trains at all, if the entire infrastructure had broken down within the country. After all, who in their right mind would volunteer to work on a train, just like any other normal day, under such circumstances? I became dubious about the possible arrival of anything other than maybe some more refugees hoping for transportation.

By noon, two trains had passed through the station – one was indeed a small local service which had just two carriages. This did not stop about two hundred people cramming themselves into every available space, some clinging to the sides, others climbing Indian style to the roof of the train.

The engine barely had enough power to pull the weight but it eventually managed to struggle out of the station. I thought there was a good chance that any other trains coming this way would be blocked by this little train broken down on the tracks a mile or so along.

The second train was considerably larger – eight carriages and all the normal guards and railway staff you would expect. The guards even wore their uniforms, acted like it was an ordinary day. It was surreal. Ten minutes later the train pulled out of the station – overloaded like the little train before it. There had been news that another longer train was on its way here, expected to arrive early afternoon. This was the train I would be getting on. If I had to trample the sick, old and dying I would be getting on that train.

As it turned out I did not have to fight to get on the train. It was crowded but not crazy crowded. I stood in a little alcove behind a luggage rack and just hung on for the four hours it took for the train to get to its destination. I had no idea what that destination was – all written signs were in Lithuanian.

When I got off the train – hot and stressed – I saw that we were in a large mainline station. I recognised the name Vilnius – the capital city of Lithuania – not far from the border with Belarus.

Here I found that signs were written not just in the local language but also in English. A fair percentage of the dwellers of this large city spoke good English. By talking to a few of them I met in the station, I found out that the wind was still blowing the atomic dust across the Atlantic towards America and it was hoped it would dissipate to a reasonable level before the air currents changed direction.

The main airport in Vilnius was operating fairly normally. Although extremely busy, it was theoretically still possible to get a flight out of the country.

I managed to get directions towards the airport but had no money or identity papers. It had not mattered

193

when I was in the far-flung countryside, or getting on emergency trains to arrive here but this city was not being abandoned – it was just extra busy. This meant that the bureaucracy was also in full working order – I could not get a train, plane or even taxi with no way of paying for it.

I decided that my most hopeful – and simultaneously my most feared option – was to try to make my way to Riga in Latvia – as per my instructions from Johnny Walsh, when I last spoke to him on the radio of my now destroyed boat *Valerie II*.

I had missed the deadline of Tuesday but thought it likely they would still be looking out for me in the approaches of the city.

Riga was almost 200 miles away from my current location – it would take me a week to walk there if I really pushed myself and if I could find the necessary food and water to keep myself alive. It was a difficult task - made even harder due to my complete lack of knowledge of the area – I had no map to point me in the correct direction. If I got lost, I could be wandering about in circles for months. There was also the problem of getting across the border into Latvia with no passport or proof of identity. I would worry about that later – if I ever got near to the border in one piece.

At least I had a goal – even a bad plan was better than no plan. My main worry was not what would happen to me if I did not reach Riga – it was what would happen to me if I *did* reach Riga.

Chapter 34

It took me ten days to get to the Latvian border – I took several extensive detours but finally I was within sight of the customs buildings. I had no idea if it was even possible for me to get across, as I had no papers, no proof of who I was, no money, no real explanation for why I wanted to cross into the country. I wouldn't have let me in if I was a border guard.

I had been convinced, after the sinking of my boat and the fact I knew not a single person in Lithuania that I had finally broken free of Walsh and his G10 psychopaths – it had been a relief.

I couldn't explain my decision to head towards the exact place I had been instructed to go, by the very people I wanted to avoid. Maybe it was an urge to get somewhere where I could access resources, find people who may have information about what was happening to the world - because they were almost certainly the ones causing it to happen. Better the devil you know, blah blah, blah…

I approached the customs guard and hoped he would speak English – my Latvian was a little rusty.

"Michael Garvie?" he asked me in better English than I could have managed myself.

I nodded.

"Please come this way – we have been expecting you!"

"You've been expecting me?" I almost laughed out loud – G10 obviously had contacts in the most obscure places.

I followed the guard along a short gravel pathway, into what looked like a small workman's hut – from the outside.

Inside it contained just a lift, with a row of buttons and lights in a panel on the wall. The guard pressed a button marked '3', an inner door slid into place.

The lift descended smoothly; the door re-opened. I was stunned by what was on level 3. It looked like Mission Control for an international space program.

There were several rows of computer screens, banks of server cabinets, stretching off into the distance. The people operating the computers wore black uniforms with a G10 insignia on the front.

I looked around the room – trying to take it all in, when a familiar voice addressed be from the right-hand side of the main walkway.

"Ahoy there, Squirrel". My legs buckled. I grabbed hold of the wall, turned in the direction of the voice. My heart was pounding, my mind reeling. Mark Hopkins stood five feet away. He wore a uniform with an elaborate insignia. He was smiling, holding out his hand. I fell on the floor before I could shake it.

When I came back to consciousness I was in a bed. The bed was in a small room. The door was closed. There was no window. A dim bulb in the ceiling shed a comfortable light onto the scene. I noticed a bedside table which had a glass of water on it, nothing else. There was a red button fitted into a small electronic panel on the wall behind my bed. I felt I was in a hospital – which I probably was. I couldn't care less. I went to sleep in a very bad mood.

I woke up in a very bad mood. A big male nurse came in which annoyed me. I like pretty little girl nurses

196

not hairy great oafs with arms like builders. He told me I could get up anytime and would be transferred into my official quarters later that morning. He sounded like a native speaker of English. There was nothing Latvian about him as far as I could ascertain. I didn't reply when he spoke to me. I went back to sleep in an incredibly bad mood.

The next time I awoke was to the sound of men talking about me. "He needs to get set up in his quarters, then a full induction session". "We need to get a move on, prepare him for the 5.30". "Maybe we should keep him here a bit longer?" "We need to get back as soon as possible".

"Oi, could you please fuck off and have your little meeting somewhere else ladies?"

"Oh, so you're awake at last?"

"I don't know – you tell me – I've been having trouble getting a grip on reality lately". Somebody found that amusing and laughed.

I sat up and opened my eyes. There were three men in the room. Mark Hopkins, Johnny Walsh – and just to add the mindfuck icing to the cake – Art Mercer.

"You lot can just go fuck yourselves!" I said in a flat voice. I stared at them but they remained visible – I had been expecting them to disappear into thin air. They just stood there – all wearing silly uniforms with logos on and some sort of army officers' caps – they looked ridiculous. I told them so. Johnny laughed. I laughed. It was ridiculous. Everything was ridiculous.

"If you've had enough kip, you can come with us – there's a lot you need to know mate" this was Mark Hopkins. The same Mark Hopkins whose body I had last seen in pieces in a warehouse in St. Malo – or a very good facsimile of his body – I was beginning to believe the craziest things – but they still weren't as crazy as the things which were actually happening. I got out of bed – I was wearing pale green pyjamas – and walked over to the men. "Lead on McDuff!"

I followed them out of the room, into a narrow grey corridor. There were several doors along both sides, each had a number. My room had been 476. This was a high number – it told me I was in a large building or 'facility'.

There was a lot more to this than just a few control freak criminals setting me up as some sort of patsy. I had no idea what I was involved in – but it was on a very large scale indeed – a fact which gave me some hope that there would be some underlying sanity beneath all the madness. But I wasn't holding my breath about that – things had been getting weirder and weirder for a few years now. I had no explanations about any of it - none which I believed at any rate. I thought maybe we were approaching the final revelation moment. It was something I wanted more than I had ever wanted anything – just for reality to make sense again – that was my only wish.

I followed my entourage into a large elevator which moved at high speed, down several levels. Then we walked out into a large forecourt area with small warehouses dotted around. There were people dressed like mechanics and technicians milling around as well as a shielded off area at the far end which had guards near the entrance to what looked like a foyer.

Inside this guarded area I was taken to a room with a bed, cabinet, television, bookcase – in fact well-appointed living quarters if you were in the military. I was told I was to occupy this room until the debriefing session which was to begin soon. There were drinks in the fridge and some pre-packed snacks.

I was then left alone and sat on the bed for a while, taking in my surroundings. I grabbed a cold drink from the fridge and a pasty of some sort which tasted bland but not unpleasant. The drink was a pale pink colour. It tasted refreshingly fruity. It was only later that I found out it was a strong sedative.

Chapter 35

I woke up in a different bed – wearing some sort of full body outfit – a kind of jump suit. A nurse – this time pleasantly female, was sitting on a chair by the side of my bed.

"Oh, so you're back with us again are you Mr. Garvie – how very nice of you to join us".

"What the hell's going on now? Who's been dressing me up and moving me about?" The nurse chuckled.

"We had to move you so you could be brought with the generals – seems you are some sort of VIP."

"No idea what you're talking about"

"You'll be put in the picture soon – induction in half an hour Sweety. I will notify them of your return to consciousness"

"Suit yourself" I quipped. She went out and closed the door behind her. Then she came back in and asked me to follow her to the conference suite. I walked along a dark corridor, until we arrived at a wide door with a metal sign on it - 'Conference Suite'. There was a G10 logo underneath the sign. I groaned.

The room was large – it had modern metal consoles around the edge of its semi-circular sides and a large window which showed a few stars but nothing else – the day had passed without me knowing much about it – I had been unconscious mostly.

A large desk was situated in front of this widow and behind the desk sitting on chairs – all dressed in fancy military uniforms were my old pals – Johnny, Mark and Art Mercer.

"Not you bastards again – is there no escape from your evil clutches?" I said this in a jokey way, though I felt anything but amused. Mark Hopkins motioned towards a chair.

"Take a seat Mike – we will explain everything to your satisfaction – there will be no more mind-games or sudden dangerous occurrences – we will put you fully in the picture"

"How reassuring. Maybe you could start by telling me where the hell I am and why you let off those nuclear bombs?" The sarcasm in my voice was obvious.

"Well for starters" Hopkins replied "we didn't let off any bombs – nuclear or otherwise"

"Oh, I must have imagined that then" They all laughed at this – it seemed the mind-games were to continue after all – I never doubted that they would.

"You must excuse us – we will let you in on the joke in a minute but first of all we would like to welcome you to your new home".

"Don't kid yourself pal, I intend to get out of Latvia as soon as I get the chance – and I hope never to see any of your ugly mugs ever again"

"You might be stuck with us a while longer" replied Hopkins "You see, Squirrel, you are currently residing on the Moon – G10 MoonBase Darkside to be precise!"

Chapter 36

My induction lasted twelve days. I was given upgraded quarters in the officers' block, reinstated as Captain in the G10 group. I learned how and why I had been manipulated – mainly I was being tested to see if I would be able to come to terms with the new reality I now found myself in.

I also learned that Mark Hopkins was a genuine good guy. In fact, he was a legend.

No nuclear bombs had gone off. News stories about nuclear explosions are not the same as actual nuclear explosions. I found out that 99% of the human race were slaves, living under powerful constructs and belief systems, imposed from beyond the earth and used to control them.

I had now been rescued from this control system, was part of a breakaway group who were fighting back against the beings – human and non-human, who had controlled our planet and manipulated its people for millennia.

After all the weird stuff that had happened to me over the past few years, it was ironic that the thing which would set me free, was finding out something even weirder. But that is what had happened. I was no longer long-term loser Mike Garvie, dabbling in contraband cigarettes, wasting my best years doing nothing in particular.

Now I was Captain Michael Garvie of the G10 Interstellar Rebel Force. I was a space soldier fighting for the very existence, not just of my home planet, Earth – but of the whole galaxy!

It was in the balance, whether the galaxy as we knew it would survive and it was up to me – and my colleagues in G10 - to determine the outcome of a war of such immense proportions as to be barely conceivable.

It was the ultimate shit or bust!

Captain Michael Garvie will return next year in

The Black Moon

204

Printed in Great Britain
by Amazon

86245181R00122